DEATH ON THE ISLE OF LOVE

Emily Queen

Death on the Isle of Love

Copyright © 2019 by Emily Queen

ISBN- 978- 1700482525

First Edition

Printed in the U.S.A.

Other Books in this series:

Table of Contents

CHAPTER ONE

"Attention, passengers. We'll be docking in Cyprus in fifteen minutes. Local time is 7:52 a.m. Please be ready to disembark promptly."

The disembodied voice sounded oddly mechanical through the loudspeaker, but Rosemary Lillywhite caught the gist of the statement. With barely contained excitement, she exchanged grins with her best friend—one of her three traveling companions—who stood alongside her on the deck waiting for their destination to come into view.

That Vera Blackburn had joined her on this tropical adventure wasn't surprising; the beautiful, spunky actress could always be counted on to come through, especially when a healthy dose of fun in any form was involved.

Rosemary's brother, Frederick, on the other hand, had finally learned to save his shenanigans for the weekends after having put in a full week's worth of work at their father's company, Woolridge & Sons.

With the death of their older brother—also Vera's first and, to her mind, one true love—Frederick had become the only male Woolridge heir, and their father impressed upon him the duty to learn every nuance of the family business. In a shocking turn of events, Freddie took his job seriously. In fact, it had taken the lingering stain of a murder investigation—with Frederick as the prime suspect—to convince him a sabbatical was in order.

Rounding out the foursome was Desmond Cooper, Frederick's longtime mate and Rosemary's childhood crush. She'd given up on the fantasy of Des a split second after she'd laid eyes on Andrew Lillywhite, but her husband's untimely death the year before had put Rose back on the market. At least, according to anyone who felt the need to comment on the situation—such as her mother and, of course, Vera. While Rosemary still got butterflies in her stomach when she was around Desmond, the thought of becoming romantically involved with a man other than her late husband turned their flight into a swarm that made her stomach ache.

Sunny days, sandy beaches, and exotic cocktails near sparkling waters had sounded far too tempting after the ordeal of clearing Frederick's good name, and Rosemary had, for once, thrown caution to the wind and decided to treat herself to a much-needed holiday.

As if her life wasn't complicated enough, there was Detective Inspector Maximilian Whittington back in London to consider. Max, a handsome fellow and a stalwart friend, had worked closely with Andrew in his private investigating enterprise and then, during Freddie's untimely brush with murder, had stepped in to help clear her brother's name.

While Rosemary had been glad of the help, she was not, as Vera continued to insist, in love with Max. Nor was she, as Vera also continued to insist, the lady who doth protest too much. Max was merely a friend, and even if the idea of a romance with him intrigued her, she considered it best to push those feelings aside. That she could do so was, in Rosemary's estimation, a sign that she wasn't ready.

Falling in love should overwhelm all of a woman's senses, not trigger her common sense. That was how it had happened with Andrew and was now the measure by which she would gauge all such experiences. Not that Rose intended to have a great many of them.

"We're finally here, Rosie," Vera squealed at a pitch that could have cut glass. "The Isle of Love, that's what they call

Cyprus you know," she said, her emerald eyes sparkling from beneath a sheaf of inky lashes.

Rosemary cocked an eyebrow at her friend. "Yes, I'm aware of the island's nickname, as you've mentioned it approximately eighty-seven times since we left London."

"It's just so beautiful, I can't stand it," Vera continued as if Rosemary hadn't said a word. "You can almost feel the romance, and we haven't even docked yet."

"There are other things in life besides men, you know."

When Vera smiled, even the sun seemed to dim a little in comparison. "Well, of course there are, dear one, but none so devilishly interesting."

"Where are Fred and Des, anyway?" Rosemary changed the subject while her eyes roamed the deck in search of her brother's head of golden curls. "What am I saying? Obviously, we'll find them—"

"Guzzling down cocktails," Vera finished for her. "And I imagine poor Anna is still in the loo, sicking up." Rosemary's maid had battled motion sickness ever since they'd boarded the train in London and had turned an ugly shade of green before the ship had even pulled completely away from the dock.

"Poor girl. She might have mentioned she didn't travel well," Rosemary said, a note of worry in her voice.

"I expect she was overcome by the excitement of a holiday. She'll come right once her feet are back on solid ground, though I do wonder if she'll spend the entire holiday dreading the return trip."

Rosemary sighed. "Or trying to talk the fair Cecily into hiring her on to avoid it."

"Speaking of, how well do you know this Cecily DeVant person?" Vera asked.

"Not at all, really, she hasn't visited England since I was quite young, and I hardly remember the occasion. Still, as many times as I have listened to Mother wax on about her oldest and dearest friend, I feel as if I know her."

Gripping the rail, Vera raised her face and leaned into the wind. "What's her story?" she said, as the breeze ruffled her hair.

9

"How did she come to be running a hotel in Cyprus of all places?"

Those details hadn't been as important to Rose's mother as passing along what she perceived as pertinent facts about the hotel.

"No idea, really. All I know is that whoever built the hotel went to great expense to make it as lavish as possible."

Rose watched with a hand at the ready to catch her friend should Vera lean too far.

"I'd have been happy to stay in any sort of place. Travel is meant to broaden one's experience, after all."

Rosemary grinned. "Oh, I daresay you'll appreciate the finer amenities on offer at the Aphrodite Sands. Mother positively gushed over the lift of all things. According to Cecily, it was a task of great endurance and expense to have it shipped over and installed. I'm sure it couldn't have taken as long as it did for Mother to tell the story."

"So long as there's sand, sun, and good gin, I can't imagine we'll lack for anything." Taking Rose by the arm, Vera turned away from the rail, and the view.

"Now," she continued, "I estimate we have another ten minutes, which leaves just enough time for one last mimosa, don't you think?"

"Lead on, but for heaven's sake, Vera, don't go that way." Having spied three elderly women arguing over deck chairs to her left, Rose dragged Vera on a circuitous route to the bar. Halfway through the first day of their voyage, Mrs. Edina Haversham discovered Vera sunning herself on the forward deck and attached herself like a leech to her favorite actress.

At every turn, she and two other fluffy dowagers sprang out of nowhere demanding Vera recite lines from one play or another.

"Your flock of admirers will see us and ask you to perform again. We'll never get our mimosa, and I don't think I could take another dramatic death scene reenactment."

"Why, Rosemary darling, I'm positively gutted. Did you not say my Desdemona was a revelation?" Vera's eyes twinkled with great humor.

"And so it was," Rose said with a grin. "The first time. Alas, with numerous repetitions, I find Desdemona pales."

Having avoided the old biddies, the pair strolled over to where Frederick and Desmond held court at the bar. Vera ordered and handed a frothy yellow drink to her friend and took a satisfying sip of her own. "These are going to be dangerous," she mused, elbowing Frederick sharply for no real reason other than to interrupt the boastful story he'd been telling the two attractive women who were hanging on his every word.

"...and then, I punched him square in the jaw—ouch!" he said, turning to Vera in surprise. "What was that for?" he asked, his voice at a slightly higher pitch than normal.

"Oh, you know. Nothing in particular." Vera's eyes sparkled prettily but with razor sharpness. She linked arms with Rosemary and walked back towards a pair of deck chairs. "He's going to get what's coming to him, that I can promise."

"When he least expects it, I'm sure," Rosemary said with a wry smile. She was used to playing referee between her brother and her best friend, whose relationship was forever fraught with conflict. Desmond nearly got his head bitten off on the train when he posited the opinion that the constant bickering smelt of romantic interest. Now, as Rose met his eyes across the platform, she knew his amused expression meant he was even more convinced of the notion than ever before. "At least this time you have a good reason for knocking him down a peg or two."

"Darned right I do," Vera agreed, recalling the moment when she and Frederick had been called upon to distract the attention of a group of corrupt gamblers. Given no further order than to create a diversion, Frederick had chosen to run his hand up her backside. His ploy, though ill-advised, had done the trick. Outraged, Vera had kicked up a fuss, but even now, she flushed at the memory of how his hand had felt on her.

"I know it was part of the covert affair, and that we took down a notorious criminal as a result, but did he really have to manhandle me to successfully create a distraction? That's right, he did not." She answered her own question before Rosemary could take a breath. "Oh, look, we're docking!" All thoughts of revenge seemed to evaporate as the boat came to a stop.

A flurry of activity on the dock from several men in crisp white shirts reminded Rosemary of a glass-encased ant farm she'd seen at a museum when she was a child. In the short time it took to disembark, each one had amassed a pile of luggage from below decks and loaded them into the small bus that would take them to the hotel.

"Mrs. Woolridge," the driver, a snazzily-dressed young man, stuttered in a British accent as Rosemary approached.

"Mrs. Woolridge is my mother," Rose replied with a half-smile. "I'm Rosemary Lillywhite, and this lot is with me." She gestured towards her friends.

The boy—for he was barely more than sixteen years old by Rose's estimation—turned a deep shade of red and apologized profusely. "I'm so sorry, Madam. So sorry. Please accept my deepest apologies."

"It's quite all right, Ustus," she said, peering at the gold-trimmed name badge pinned somewhat awkwardly onto his shirt. "No harm done. You'll find we're an easygoing lot, save for my brother the troublemaker, but I'll tip you handsomely at the end of the trip if you ignore him completely." She winked and young Ustus sighed with relief.

The bus ride to the hotel was long, dusty, and more than a little jarring given the condition of the road, which went unnoticed as the scenery commanded the attention of the group.

Groves of citrus and ripening olive trees, their trunks a fascination of twisting shapes, flanked parts of the road from the village, the scent of oranges and lemons riding the warm air like a blessing. There were, Rosemary noted, far more trees than buildings, yet she wouldn't describe the landscape as primitive or untamed.

Ustus kept up a running commentary that Rose let flow past her without listening too closely. Her artist's eye was too busy making impressions and memorizing shapes and colors to be turned into sketches later. Locals in traditional garb blended with Brits wearing current fashions to create a wealth of pattern and movement.

Vera, of course, concentrated on the male population, while Frederick kept his eye on the female. Des, as was his way, said very little.

Over the crest of a low hill, the Aphrodite Sands Hotel finally came into view, its whitewashed facade and modern architecture standing out in stark contrast from everything they'd seen along the way. With bated breath, the foursome emerged from the bus and approached the front entrance. Stone steps cut into perfect rectangles and buffed to a gleaming shine spanned the width of the hotel, potted ferns and colorful plants dotting the expanse.

Rosemary fingered a rubbery leaf and bent her head to sniff the single flower blossoming from one of its tendrils. Yes, she was going to have a nice, relaxing holiday surrounded by the type of exotic beauty London simply couldn't boast. She only wished she'd packed some canvas and her paints but settled instead for committing the scene to memory.

She trailed behind her companions, who hadn't taken the time to stop and soak in the atmosphere, and approached the front counter at the rear of the group. Vera shot her a look from beneath furrowed brows as the receptionist, a petite, pinch-faced Greek woman with curly black hair leafed through a leather-bound register.

"I'm sorry," she said, not sounding sorry at all, "but I can only seem to find two rooms listed under the name Woolridge."

"Try Lillywhite," Rosemary said, pushing between Frederick and Vera.

Rose's jovial mood plummeted while the receptionist scanned through the names listed on the page again. "I am sorry. If you would wait one moment," she said, and without any explanation turned and strode away. After a few minutes, she returned with another woman in tow.

"Well, I'll be—" The second woman stopped to gaze at Rosemary.

This, Rose decided, could be none other than Cecily DeVant. It wasn't the English accent or the familiarity with which the woman spoke that created such certainty; it was the description that her mother had given Rosemary before she left

13

London. When Evelyn Woolridge had said her friend was the 'oddest looking woman' she'd ever met, Rose had taken the statement with a grain of salt.

Evelyn still couldn't wrap her mind around why not all women focused on their looks or aspired to no greater heights than marrying well, so her perspective tended to be somewhat one-dimensional.

However, in this instance, it seemed her mother had not missed the mark at all. Cecily's face was a contradiction of angles. Impossibly high cheekbones created a triangular effect between her eyes and mouth, the features as symmetrical as those of an Egyptian princess. That is if you could look beyond the prominent, arrow-straight nose that angled towards the left side of her face so abruptly it gave Rosemary a start.

"You must be Rosemary," she trilled, stepping forward with her arms outstretched. "You're the spitting image of your mother when she was a girl. It's striking, as a matter of fact," Cecily said, cocking her head to one side as she made her appraisal.

"Yes," Rosemary smiled. She couldn't help but take an instant liking to the woman, though her mother had mentioned getting on Cecily's bad side was inadvisable, and Rose had no doubt the statement was true. Formidable, be she friend or foe, was a fitting word for Cecily DeVant. "You must be Cecily. It's a pleasure to meet you again." Rosemary held out a hand but was instead enveloped in a lavender-scented embrace.

"We'll have to take lunch together sometime during your stay. I have many stories about your mother I think you'll find amusing," Cecily said, her gaze having come upon Frederick during the conversation. "And you look too much like your father not to be Cecil's son." He was treated to an enthusiastic hug, which Frederick returned in kind.

"Cecil and Cecily," he said, grinning and shaking his head. "I can only imagine how confusing that was for Mother."

Cecily laughed. "Perhaps, though the only thing I ever heard her call your father was 'darling' or 'dear' or some other such term of endearment. Are they still as besotted with each other as they once were?"

Rosemary detected a hint of jealousy in Cecily's tone, not that she could blame her. It wasn't easy being a third wheel, as Rose had learned since becoming a single woman for the second time in her life.

Frederick assured her that their parents were still happily married and then introduced Cecily to Vera and Desmond. Once pleasantries had been exchanged to her satisfaction, she retreated to the other side of the counter and took a look at the ledger.

"Gloria, honestly!" Cecily admonished the receptionist, whose face went a deep shade of scarlet. "Could I have made it any easier for you to reserve the proper number of rooms? I distinctly remember writing you a note explaining that the Woolridge-Lillywhite party would need two suites plus a room for their staff. That's three rooms, and you only reserved two," she continued even though the public shaming of an employee made everyone feel somewhat uncomfortable. Anna hung back, a look of pure mortification on her round little face.

"I'm sorry." Gloria dropped her eyes, but not before Rose detected mutiny in her expression. "Margaret saw the note and passed the information along to me, but one of us must have made a mistake. All the suites are filled. Should I ask one of the other guests to change rooms?"

Desmond stepped forward and cleared his throat loudly. "No need to trouble yourself, really. Frederick and I will do just as well in the smaller room." He received a nod from Rosemary, and a small, grateful smile from the receptionist, who peered at him with interest.

"Yes," Rosemary said, "and Anna will stay in our suite, right, Vera?" Vera nodded her agreement.

"Very well, but your graciousness doesn't let Gloria off the hook." Cecily continued to berate the woman, whose face had gone stony. Her eyes brimmed with unshed tears.

"You're lucky I don't let you go, Gloria." Cecily's tone insinuated this wasn't the first such mistake the girl had made. "We'll discuss this further later." She took her leave, citing urgent hotel business, and Gloria breathed a sigh of relief at her departure.

Rosemary thought once more how her mother had been right—one certainly didn't want to get on Cecily DeVant's bad side.

CHAPTER TWO

"I'm sorry we all have to share a suite, Miss Rose," Anna said quietly while they waited for the porter to load the luggage onto a rolling cart. "I'll sleep on the floor; there's no need for you and Miss Vera to share a bed."

Rosemary sighed and brushed a lock of hair away from Anna's face. "You'll do no such thing. It's not your fault, dear, and furthermore, it's of no concern. We'll have a grand time all together. It will be like a slumber party. Vera and I have shared a bed plenty of times over the years. She hardly snores at all."

Vera aimed a mock-angry glare at her friend.

"Besides, we won't be spending much time in the suite anyway, and Fred and Des will be just fine sharing a smaller room." The girl appeared slightly mollified, and Rosemary wondered if she would ever convince Anna to stop worrying so much.

While they waited, the famously imported lift returned to the first floor. A balding man of advanced age stepped off and rudely pressed between Rosemary and Vera without so much as a glance of apology. As he approached the reception desk with a stormy expression on his pinched face, the look on Gloria's made it clear she'd prefer being drawn and quartered to dealing with him.

"What is it now, Mr. Wright?" she asked with a nearly audible roll of her eyes that didn't go unnoticed by the cranky gentleman.

"You'd best think twice before speaking to me in that tone, Missy," the man snarled. "Is it *my* fault your staff is hopelessly inept? Where is Miss DeVant? I'd like to have a word with her about the maid service, as well as your behavior. A high-class hotel like this having hired incompetents to run the place. It's a damn shame, that's what it is." He paused for a moment and continued to glare at Gloria before demanding once more, "Where is Miss DeVant?"

Gloria's eyes narrowed dangerously. "She's indisposed at the moment, dealing with more important matters than your petty complaints. We've been more than accommodating to your requests, Mr. Wright, but even Miss DeVant has a limit. I'll be sure to pass along the message." She said the last with another roll of her eyes.

"You do that," Mr. Wright snapped, "and while you're at it, remind her I am still trying to contact the owner of this establishment. I intend to file a formal complaint."

"The owner won't talk to you," Gloria replied, her voice just as icy as his. "Ever. So, you might as well stop hounding Miss DeVant."

Mr. Wright smirked. "We'll see about that. We'll just see. I expect my message will be received in a timely manner." He strutted in the direction of the breakfast bar and missed the daggered look Gloria aimed at his back.

Rose observed the exchange with a mixture of horror and interest until her attention turned to the porter. She watched as he piled Vera's many cases onto the cart in a precise configuration with hardly any gaps. He bit his lip as he loaded the last one and grinned to nobody, Rose could ascertain, but himself.

"Thank you," she said. "That's quite a stack, isn't it? I'm afraid we have a habit of packing rather heavily." Rosemary glanced at Vera, but her friend showed no sign of remorse.

"I might not pack lightly," Vera mumbled, "but I'm always ready for all contingencies."

"Yes, Madam," the porter mumbled, a blush rising in his cheeks. "It's no problem. Miss DeVant says I can take two trips if I have to, but..." he trailed off as if he didn't know quite how to finish his sentence. "I'm Benny. Follow me and I will show you to your rooms." He smiled shyly and then lumbered off, pushing the cart towards the lift, where he squeezed past the operator.

It was a tight fit with the four of them plus Benny, the operator, and the luggage, and everyone held their breath as they ascended to the top floors of the hotel. Frederick and Desmond were first deposited into their smaller shared room one floor down from the women and agreed to meet them in the lounge after everyone had freshened up.

"Here we are," Benny declared as the door to the lift opened on the next floor up. He pushed his cart towards the suite marked 303. "Mr. Wright, whom you...er met downstairs, is just down the hall in 305. There are only three suites on this level. They're the nicest ones we offer here at Aphrodite Sands." That part sounded rehearsed. "You can even call down to the reception desk from your room."

"It's a nice hotel and I can see Cecily works hard to provide all the most modern amenities," Rose said, her gaze wandering around the lavish suite.

"Yes, Miss. Still, the elevator don't always run just right, and there's an echo effect on the stairs." Benny pulled a brass cigarette lighter from his pocket and absently spun the flint to produce a flicker of flame. "Miss Cecily says it's to do with the angles and curves of the walls, but noises come right up sometimes."

When Rosemary stepped further into the suite amid Vera's squeals of delight and Anna's soft exclamations, she felt as though she'd been transported to another world. Windows spanned the wall across from the entrance door, opening onto a balcony that overlooked the brolly-dotted beach and provided a breathtaking view of the sea and mountains beyond. Intricately carved woodwork spanned from floor to waist height and continued in the crown molding and ceiling, the wall between covered with fabric wallpaper that looked like hand-spun silk.

19

All the furnishings were of the highest quality, with a sunken sitting area taking up the center of the main room. Through the twin doors on either side, two large four-poster beds piled with pillows promised the experience of sleeping on a cloud. Even Vera, who had traveled far and wide and stayed in some of the most expensive hotels money could buy, was taken aback by the sheer luxury by which she, Rosemary, and Anna were now surrounded.

As he wheeled the cart into the room, Benny went into a rehearsed spiel about the hotel and how the management spared no expense to provide features found nowhere else on the island, including en-suite bathrooms and hot running water. He didn't mention the lift again, but he did add in his more normal cadence of speech that the boiler worked most of the time and the water was never rusty.

"Thank you, Benny," Rosemary said after he'd unloaded the cart. "You've been most helpful."

The man blushed again, mumbled something along the lines of "if you ladies need anything else…" then trailed off and beat a hasty retreat out the door.

Once he had gone, Rosemary flopped onto the bed and let out a giggle. "It's even better than I imagined. I could stay here all day eating chocolates and taking in the view."

"Well, Rosie dear, I have a feeling that's what we'll be doing the day after Desmond convinces us to hike up one of those mountains," Vera said, her voice taking on a tired-sounding tone at the mere thought of physical exertion.

"We'll cross that bridge when—and *if*—we come to it," Rosemary said with a laugh. "For now, I'm going to take a nice, long bath and hope my brother hasn't gone three sheets to the wind before we make it down for tea. It's quite early yet, but that's never stopped him before."

She rose and peeked into Anna's room, where the girl lay sprawled out on the fluffy down mattress. She gave a contented sigh. "It's not moving," she said with a yawn. "I think I shall stay here and unpack rather than go down for tea, if that's all right."

"Ring down and see if one of the hotel staff can bring you something," Rosemary suggested. "I wish I could do the same,

20

but the men are expecting us to rally. I refuse to be called a stick in the mud. You know how Freddie can get when he feels we aren't upholding our sacred duty to enjoy ourselves."

Anna smiled and nodded as she spotted the telephone on a table with a card lying next to it. "Oh, look here's a menu. Isn't that simply topping." She scanned the sheet, her eyes widening at the selection, and she said on a breath, "There's too much to choose from, and they're all dishes I recognize." Once underway, Anna had fretted about having to eat things that might make her sick. "Should I order a scone or cake?"

"Get both, then, and enjoy yourself." It didn't take much to make Anna happy, and for all the little things she did to please her mistress, Rosemary wanted nothing more than to ensure she had the time of her life on the Isle of Love. The grin on Anna's face was thanks enough.

While the tub filled with the hottest water Rosemary could stand, she tossed in a handful of bath salts, then stepped out onto the balcony and surveyed her surroundings. She'd kept a morsel of information from even her best friend; Cyprus was a place Rosemary and her late husband Andrew had dreamed of visiting. Being here without him was bittersweet, but it was something she needed to endure to move on. As long as this holiday went off without a hitch, she believed she'd find herself stronger at the end of it. With one last lingering look at the beauty surrounding her, Rosemary strode back inside towards the fragrant bath that promised to soothe all her rough edges.

CHAPTER THREE

An hour later, she and Vera, dressed for tea in light, gauzy frocks, passed Anna stashing the luggage in a coat cupboard near the door as they exited the suite, and pressed the button to summon the lift. Their wait was interrupted by the uttered expletives of a man entering the hallway from suite 301, the room across the hall that Rose was sure must have been meant for Frederick and Desmond before the receptionist's error.

"Sodding porter," he muttered before he realized he had an audience. "Oh, hello," he said, looking up and eying both she and Vera with obvious interest. "You must be new to the floor. I'm sure I would have remembered seeing two stunning beauties such as yourselves wandering about."

Under normal circumstances, it might have come across as charming, but something about the man rubbed Rosemary the wrong way. Perhaps it was the sneer that had passed his face before he realized he had an audience; or perhaps it was the way his gaze didn't quite make it north of her neck. She could tell her friend felt the same way because Vera stiffened beside her.

"Charmed, I'm sure," Rosemary replied, and then shifted her eyes to the lift door, praying it would open soon and rescue them.

The man laughed and looked at Vera conspiratorially. "I get the impression your companion doesn't care for me, and we've only just met. I have been told I'm an acquired taste," he boomed

22

proudly and reached forward to jab at the lift button even though the light indicating it was on its way was already lit.

We should have looked for the stairs, Rose thought when their unwanted companion offered an opinion on what not to see and do during their stay.

Rosemary sighed with relief when he exited on the second floor.

"What an utter cad," Vera said, shrugging off the unpleasant encounter.

By the time the pair arrived back in the lobby, they were good and ready to sample the offerings at the hotel's much-touted lounge. Mouthwatering scents wafted towards them from the lounge entrance.

"I'm famished," Vera said, sniffing the air. "What do you suppose smells so delicious?"

Rose's stomach rumbled in response. "I have no idea, but I hope Freddie forgoes his habit of being fashionably late. I'm too hungry to wait."

She needn't have worried, she thought as she spotted Freddie holding court at the bar with Desmond by his side. The two stood from the barstools they'd been leaning against, tossed back the rest of their drinks, and rushed forward.

"It's about time the two of you finished primping." Frederick's voice slurred slightly, and he swayed a little as he approached the hostess station.

Rosemary cocked an eyebrow at him. "We're here now, Freddie," she said lightly, "and it appears you could use a little something to soak up all those mimosas." If there was an edge to her voice, Frederick pretended not to notice while he made a vow to consume as many mimosas as his stomach could handle. He was, after all, on holiday. If Rose wanted to spend her time acting responsibly, that was her choice, but he would behave exactly as he pleased.

"What do you think about the hotel?" Rosemary aimed her question at Desmond, who had said very little thus far. He appeared to have watched the exchange between the two siblings with some humor, but declined to comment.

He smiled and glanced around, taking in the intricate woodwork that spanned from floor to ceiling and echoed the feel of the top-floor suite. "It's beautiful here. You might have a hard time getting me back on the ship." It was a sentiment they all shared.

Having cleared the contents of his plate in record time, Freddie tapped his foot impatiently while he waited for the others to finish. He was itching to dip his toes in the cerulean water and didn't hesitate to let the rest of them know it.

"If I choke to death, you're going to feel just terrible, brother dear," Rosemary warned, aiming a kick to his shin.

"She's right, you know," came a high-pitched voice from behind Rosemary's chair. "Your mother would have a conniption if she heard you were mistreating your sister," Cecily's voice carried enough mirth for Frederick to know she was pulling his leg.

"Don't tell her about the frog I plan to plant in Rose's handbag, then," he replied cheerily.

Cecily grimaced and laid a hand on Rose's shoulder. "One would think he'd have learned not to tempt the fates, don't you agree?"

"Undoubtedly," Rose replied, her tone dry. "Yet somehow he never does."

"Oh," Frederick said, his eyes sparkling as he clutched his heart. "you wound me, dear sister."

Cecily's hand rested on Rosemary's shoulder in a motherly gesture. "I do hope you've had a chance to settle in and that you're finding the staff satisfactory."

Vera returned Cecily's greeting. "Everyone has been lovely so far. That porter of yours is quite a character."

"Benny? Yes, that's an apt description." Cecily's eyes flicked to the set of glass doors that opened into the lobby. "I hope he didn't talk your ear off. He tends to be garrulous at times, always asking questions, but he has a sweet nature." A soft smile suggested Cecily carried a certain fondness for the boy.

"Hardly," Rose replied. "You've got quite the place here. Mother seems to think you've finally found your calling."

Cecily laughed again. It seemed like something she did on almost as frequent a basis as sternly lecturing her staff on proper workplace behavior. The woman was a living contradiction.

"I believe I have. When my uncle decided to spend an absolute fortune building a luxury hotel here, the rest of my family decided he'd lost his faculties." She shrugged. "I thought it was a splendid idea and insisted he cut me in on the deal, and moreover, that I should move here and run the place myself."

"Heavens, mother never said you owned the hotel."

"She wouldn't, as I haven't told her, or anyone else, really. I've had to deal with enough speculation as the manager; think what would happen if people knew I owned the place. As I shall, since my uncle never married, and has already made provisions for his portion to come to me when he is gone."

No wonder Cecily took such pains to ensure the guests received only the highest quality treatment.

"Oh, bother."

Cecily cut the conversation short when she spied something out of the corner of her eye. "Excuse me, dear ones, I must go do my job now." She bustled across the dining room and spoke furtively to one of the buffet attendants, who glared at her back once Cecily had finished admonishing him for whatever infraction he'd committed. It didn't appear that Miss DeVant was an easy woman to work for, though Rosemary suspected that attention to detail was what had already made a name for the hotel. Business certainly boomed.

"That one's a firecracker," Vera said, watching Cecily bustle across the dining room. "I like her."

"You're in good but small company," Frederick said as he leaned in conspiratorially. "It seems the staff all detest her. I heard the bartender refer to her as *the bloody dragon*."

"I don't suppose," Rosemary said, giving Freddie a level stare, "being a woman in a position of authority is an easy thing here. Do you, dear brother?" Vera mimicked her friend's expression.

Freddie might have been more than a linen cupboard full of sheets to the wind, but he'd have to be dead stupid to argue that point with those two women. All the alcohol on the island couldn't take him down that path.

Rosemary decided she could sit at the edge of the sea and watch people come and go all day, particularly with her friends' commentary to amuse her.

Crystalline waters slid over pale sand like a lover's touch while the sun heated legs revealed by the skimpiest bathing costume Vera could talk her into buying. Rosemary determined to let all her troubles slip into the water and drift out to sea.

"This isn't what we ordered, I'm afraid," Frederick complained to the waiter, who sighed in irritation. Rosemary couldn't blame him; the sun was hot and carrying food and drink across the beach probably wasn't as fun as it might have seemed when he applied for the position.

With a weary glance at his order book, he replied, "It might be a while, but I'll be back as soon as I can," and took off at a clip.

Rosemary closed her eyes and pulled her hat back over her face while Frederick scowled at the waiter's retreating back and sipped at his gin anyway. "I know Cecily tries her best, but not all of the staff are on their toes. Should he ever come back, do you think it's worth seeing if the young man could fetch us something to eat? I'm feeling a bit peckish."

"You've got to be joking," Rosemary replied without opening her eyes. "We had tea no more than two hours ago. Besides, this heat saps my appetite. It feels lovely, though."

"Why don't we visit the village then? We can get a good look at the locals, you ladies can do some shopping, and us men can eat street fare to our heart's content," Frederick suggested excitedly.

Vera slipped her sunglasses off her nose and peered at Rosemary. "That sounds great to me. What do you think, Rose?"

"I'm in if everyone else wants to go," she said, looking at Desmond with a raised eyebrow.

He smiled and shrugged. "As if I would dare argue with the whims of women. Or Freddie here. I do have to sleep in the same room with him, and I don't need him resorting to infantile school pranks. However, I happen to agree with the ladies that I couldn't possibly eat right now."

"Wimp," Freddie said and elbowed his friend.

"Careful, Des. He'll short-sheet your bed the second you're distracted," Rose said as she donned a loose day frock to cover her suit and gathered her things. "Can we stop back up at the hotel? I don't want to carry this big bag around if we're going to be walking." She hefted an overfilled tote onto her shoulder.

"I second that," Vera said, struggling with her own load.

Rosemary snorted. "What am I thinking? Des, be a dear and flag down one of the staff."

Before Desmond could saunter off, a man who looked overly warm in his tan suit jacket approached their section of beach. "What seems to be the trouble here, folks?" he asked, causing Rosemary to start. It dawned on her a second later that he was referring to their problem with the waiter and the botched drinks.

"Oh, nothing too urgent, chap," Frederick said, his irritation at receiving the wrong order having dissipated in his excitement to explore the village. "We would, however, appreciate it if you'd take our bags back to our rooms."

The suited man's eyes narrowed, and he puffed up his chest. "I'll send one of the attendants right over, sir. Are you sure your waiter was satisfactory? As the assistant manager, you see, my goal is to bring our service up to par with the finest hotels in London or Paris. We've gone to extraordinary lengths to create an oasis of luxury."

Rosemary realized the reason for his attitude before Frederick did; the man held a position of authority and didn't appreciate being asked to perform a menial task such as carting bags to and fro.

"Thank you for asking," she said and looked at his name badge. "Walter. We're quite all right, my brother is simply picky about the ratio of his gin and tonics. We're having a lovely time."

He seemed to relax a bit, and Rosemary noted that without the furrowed brow, he appeared much younger than she'd assumed at first glance. So young, in fact, his status as a senior staff member struck her as unusual. Particularly, considering that

27

he had a hard time keeping his face from telegraphing his emotions when dealing with difficult customers. She made a mental note to have a conversation with Cecily at her earliest convenience and, given his prickly attitude, felt no remorse for ratting out young Walter.

True to his word, Walter had a young attendant there within moments, and the group prepared to spend the afternoon amongst the locals, their load significantly lighter. They meandered down the beach where, according to the map Rose had studied on the train, a trail would lead to the village.

Once the throng of bathing suit-clad holiday goers thinned, the atmosphere turned quite peaceful, and when they approached a rocky outcrop that separated one section of beach from the next, not one of the four could resist the urge to explore.

"Quite the view from up here," Freddie urged, having climbed to the top of the highest boulder. "Someone's been having a little bonfire down there." He pointed to the other side of the rock, took a few steps, and then disappeared behind it.

After a moment, his head popped back into sight. "If you don't mind scrambling over the rocks, we can go straight down from here. Or if you go that way, there's an easier path just there."

They opted to take the short climb. "Mind you step left off the last outcropping," Freddie advised, "or you'll land right in the middle of a dog's bathroom."

The rest of the group trooped after him, the girls refusing Desmond's offer of a hand in assistance. "We're more than capable of climbing over a few boulders, Des," Vera chided right before she nearly blundered into the very mess that Frederick had warned her about.

He responded by laughing and holding his hands up in surrender. "So sorry to have insulted your sense of female empowerment."

Once she'd managed to reach the other side, Rosemary realized that someone had indeed taken advantage of the private space. A ring of smaller rocks encircled a pile of charred wood, set in front of a boulder with a conveniently smooth edge she imagined would be the perfect spot to sit back and watch the flames dance against the backdrop of the rolling sea.

"When the tide is out, I bet you can reach this without the climb if you come around the beachside," Desmond commented. "Perhaps we'll take a trip back this way some evening."

Frederick wholeheartedly agreed. "Perhaps with a couple of women on our arms."

"Perhaps," Desmond said, watching Rosemary, who was still busy taking in the view.

Meanwhile, Freddie climbed back up on the boulders and picked his way to the highest point. Shading his eyes, he searched for the path to the village. Seeing none, he descended once again.

"Seems a deuced amount of walking, as there's nothing in the distance that looks remotely village-like. What say we return to the hotel and put off the excursion until the morrow?"

"Would it be too much trouble, Frederick Woolridge, if just once, you could make up your mind?" Vera's acerbic question and Freddie's absent response exemplified the hallmarks of their relationship, though neither would have appreciated the observation.

"You really should have worn a hat, Freddie," Rosemary admonished her brother upon their return, peering at his forehead, which had pinked up under the sun. "Walking around isn't the same as sitting under a sun brolly. That's going to hurt later."

They'd just reached the lobby of the hotel, and none amongst them could claim they weren't exhausted after an exciting but tiring day that seemed as though it might never end.

"Yes, Mother," Frederick replied sarcastically and poked Rosemary in the ribs. She swatted his hand away and practically pushed him out of the lift when it reached his and Desmond's floor. "Don't be late for dinner," he called over his shoulder.

CHAPTER FOUR

Rosemary awoke the next morning to the sound of knocking on the suite door, and for a moment couldn't figure out where she was. She grinned at the sight of the sunlight peeking through the drapes and hopped out of bed to open the door for the hotel maid. It seemed a touch out of the norm for the girl to be stopping by so early in the day especially considering the sign on the door clearly stated, "do not disturb," but Rosemary let her in anyhow and roused a grumbling Vera from sleep.

"I can come back if you're still sleeping, Miss," the maid said when she took in Rose's disheveled appearance.

"No, no. Come on in," Rose replied, slightly annoyed but trying hard to keep the irritation out of her voice. "We need nothing at the moment, but you can make up the beds if you'd like."

"All right," the maid replied. "I'm Charlotte. Holler if you need anything else." She approached the bed and then, instead of simply making it up as Rose had instructed, stripped the blankets and sheets and tossed them into a pile on the floor.

Anna had come out of her part of the suite and watched Charlotte with wide, incredulous eyes. When the girl moved on to her room before remaking Rosemary's bed, Anna's expression turned sour. Like a hawk, she watched while the maid did her duties, but didn't say anything. If her mistress was unhappy with the service, Rose would make the necessary complaints herself. That didn't mean, however, that Anna intended to keep quiet entirely.

"I can't believe her," she exclaimed once Charlotte had retreated with her loaded cart and was safely out of earshot. "And I really can't believe that Miss DeVant allows for that kind of service. When I was a chambermaid at the London Grand, we were held to a much higher standard. In fact, it was drilled into our heads that we were to be neither seen nor heard. She should have left when she realized you weren't ready and come back when we were all gone. That's the proper way."

It was more than Anna usually had to say, and it surprised Rosemary to hear the timid girl speak so candidly. Vera laughed, though her voice sounded thicker than usual. "They can't all be like you, Anna dear," she said with affection. "Though I have to say, I agree with you. I could have slept another hour, at least."

"She must be new, that's the only explanation. New, and improperly trained," Anna continued, her brow still furrowed in irritation. She believed that whether one enjoyed their job or not, one ought at least to do it properly. Not that she had any complaints about her own employment; Rosemary took great care of her, and she realized exactly how lucky she was. It made her want to go above and beyond, which in turn earned Rosemary's favor. A symbiotic relationship, not that Anna would have put it in those words, that pleased them both. Charlotte, on the other hand, didn't appear to possess the same sort of drive to please. For what reason, Anna couldn't guess, but she was intrigued and vowed to watch the girl carefully.

"Do you have any plans for today, Anna?" Rose asked, changing the subject. With less to do for her mistress, the girl could enjoy a half-holiday, at least. Anna assured her she'd arranged to meet up with some people she'd met down on the beach the evening before and tottered off to ready herself, forgetting about Charlotte as other, more pleasant thoughts invaded her mind. "Unless, of course, you need me," she said, almost as an afterthought.

Rosemary brushed the suggestion aside. "Nonsense, Anna dear. The staff is quite capable of caring for our basic needs. The

31

only thing I'd like is for you to try to keep our personal possessions organized; you know how messy Vera gets with her wardrobe, and her ill concern for her belongings always seems to extend to my own." Rosemary aimed a sideways look at Vera, but as usual, it contained more mirth than irritation.

How the woman managed to get away with acting the way she did was beyond Rosemary's comprehension, but she guessed it had something to do with the kind heart that lay beneath the seeming insensitivity. "Otherwise, you're free to do as you please. We are on holiday, after all, and I want you to enjoy yourself. Just be careful."

Anna thanked her mistress profusely, dressed and readied herself quickly, and went on her way after bidding Rosemary and Vera goodbye. The spring in her step brought a smile to Rosemary's face, but evidently, Vera had a different opinion on the subject.

"Mark my words, that girl has met a boy she fancies," Vera said once Anna exited the suite. She sneezed, a dainty noise that sounded more like the squeak of a mouse, and her eyes widened. "I do hope I'm not catching cold. We've only just arrived!" she said, and then returned to the subject at hand. "Did you notice how prettily Anna made herself up? I do hope she's careful." Had Vera realized just how maternal she sounded, it would have shocked her to the core.

"She's a big girl," Rosemary assured, "She can handle herself, and God help the man who tries to take advantage of her with Freddie and Des around. I fear we'd have to defend my brother's good name a second time."

Vera nodded. "Yes, I suppose you're right. He certainly can be quite chivalrous. When he feels like it, of course. Still, the men here aren't like the men at home, and Anna is young enough yet not to see the difference."

Rosemary thought about that for a moment and found the notion more concerning than she had before. It might have been Vera's flair for the dramatic, but she wasn't wrong that Anna was still quite naive when it came to the workings of men. "Perhaps you're right," she sighed. "We'll need to keep our eyes on her, but there's nothing much to be done about it right this very moment. How much trouble could she really get into?"

"Plenty," Vera snorted. "I realize you were the picture of propriety at her age, but times have changed. Luckily, you have me. I can smell a love affair from a mile away."

Rose found it amusing that her friend considered herself schooled in that area but failed to notice the romance burgeoning right beneath her very nose. She supposed it had something to do with people being able to see clearly the entanglements of others while remaining blind to their own.

Determined not to worry about Anna any more than absolutely necessary, the women readied themselves for another day amongst the sunshine and olive trees.

A lazy afternoon ushered in the evening while Rosemary and her friends lounged on the beach. She watched as a group of children splashed around in the warm seawater, thoroughly enjoying themselves and causing a tiny ache in her chest. Children were one of life's great gifts, and she was no longer sure if she'd be blessed with any. Still, she enjoyed watching them while they ran back and forth with boundless energy.

It didn't seem to matter that, due to the diverseness of the island guests, several of the little ones spoke different languages; they appeared unhampered by the barrier of language, all laughing jovially together. Rosemary thought the world would be a much better place if adults could come to the same sort of understanding.

When they finally packed up and headed inside, it was nearly dinner time, so once again, the women were expected to hurry up and meet the men at the bar. Vera scowled at Freddie the third time he reminded them to hurry and nearly shoved him out of the lift when it stopped on his floor.

"She's going to hurt you, Fred, if you don't leave off," Desmond warned with a laugh. The operator closed the doors on Frederick's response, which was probably for the best.

Up one more floor they went, Rosemary relishing the thought of removing her shoes and taking a long soak in the tub despite her brother's urge for speed. "Hold the door," a voice called just as the gate closed once more. "Oh, bother," Cecily said with a frown that turned upside down when she realized who was standing in the hallway.

"Rosemary, dear, how are you enjoying your stay?" Cecily included Vera in her query with a wide smile in the woman's direction.

"Very much, indeed," Rose replied.

Vera snorted and leaned in conspiratorially. "So much so that we may never go back home!"

"That's what I like to hear," Cecily said as she pressed the button to summon the lift. "I'll be standing here for fifteen minutes before he returns," she grimaced, swapping a slim envelope of a purse that didn't quite coordinate with her casual outfit from one hand to the other. "I suppose I ought to take the stairs. You dear young things have a wonderful evening."

"Wait," Rosemary replied as Cecily made for the stairwell. "Why don't you come in for a drink?" she offered.

Cecily raised an eyebrow and then let out one of her tinkling laughs. "I wouldn't dream of turning down that offer."

Once inside, she set the purse down next to the bar cart and served all three of them dirty martinis as though tending bar was part of her job description.

"I was sorry to hear about your loss, Rosemary," Cecily said, referring to Rosemary's late husband. "From what I'd heard, the two of you were quite the couple. A private investigator, your mother said he was."

"Yes," Rosemary replied, "he was. He was a wonderful man, and the world is a darker place without him. Life goes on, though, does it not?"

Cecily nodded, her eyes taking on a faraway expression as though she might know more about tragic losses than she let on. "It certainly does," she said lightly, and then abruptly changed the subject to Rosemary's mother.

Once Rose had assured her that her mother was thriving, Cecily proceeded to tell one or two childhood stories upon her friend. The kind dear Evelyn might have wished never to come to her daughter's ears.

"— and once we were safely on the other side of the fence, Evvie pelted the poor groundsman with the rest of the green apples she'd tucked into her skirts. Lucky for us, I suppose, as I'm sure we'd have become quite sick from eating them."

Thankful for the rare glimpse of her mother as a young girl, Rosemary asked for more stories until Cecily declared it was time to get back to work.

"That horrid estate agent Mr. Wright is just full of complaints this evening. He's requested my presence in his room so many times you'd think he was trying to seduce me." Cecily laughed at the image of herself cozying up to the plump, bald-headed man.

"He does seem rather demanding," Rosemary agreed.

Cecily snorted. "More than demanding, and he's been here for weeks, pestering my staff and me to our wit's end."

Vera snorted. "At least he's a guest rather than one of the staff. He'll have to check out eventually, won't he?"

At that, Cecily threw back her head and laughed. "I'll drink to that!" she said and lifted her glass before downing the last of the martini in one gulp.

"In my line of work, I wake up in strange hotel rooms more often than my own bed." Vera said, waving her tumbler towards Cecily, "so you must take it as a compliment when I tell you that you have turned the Aphrodite Sands into a fine establishment."

Nodding her head, Cecily thanked Vera, then went on to say, "We're a bit short-staffed at the moment. Two of our maids left us recently to get married. We seem to have had a run on holiday goers striking up a romance with the staff. Our second porter took a tumble on the beach and needs another few days to recover, and Gloria is sharing the bulk of the receptionist duties with the other girl, Margaret, and we've had to train one of the buffet attendants to man the desk during the slower times."

Vera made sympathetic noises and Rose patted Cecily's hand. "One would hardly notice the lack."

"You're too kind. I know poor Charlotte falls down on her duties. She's something of a lost soul, and I've had to make certain allowances for her, though I do expect a great deal from all of my people. Hotel of Lost Souls might have been a more apt name for the place, as we seem to attract workers with tragic pasts."

Cecily fell silent for a rare unguarded moment, and her face fell into lines of the worry and fatigue she kept carefully hidden. *The poor thing*, Rose thought, *she's working herself half to death.*

"You do find the work rewarding, Cecily? Mother will ask how I've found you, and I'd like to be able to report back that you're happy."

"What?" Cecily put a hand to her hair. "Oh, yes. I'm sorry if I've given you the wrong impression. I love my work, and this hotel has become home to me, the workers like family, foibles and all. It's just a frightful amount of work sometimes dealing with so many people. Not all of our guests are so easy to please as you."

"Yes, the irascible Mr. Wright," Vera's lips twisted, and she shook her head. "He who wishes to contact the owner and make his complaints directly. How shocked he would be to learn he already has."

"Oh," Cecily smiled conspiratorially, "Mr. Wright has an ulterior motive of which he is certain I am unaware. He'd be even more shocked to learn I know exactly why he remains immured in a suite in a hotel he insists is not up to his standards."

Always one to relish a juicy piece of gossip, Vera encouraged Cecily to spill the details. "Do tell."

"Now, now, you know it wouldn't be seemly to tell tales on a guest. Not even one as frustrating as he. Still, one does what one must." Cecily smiled. "Now, I must get back to work. Thank you, ladies, for lightening my mood. It would be lovely if neither of *you* had to check out. Have a good night!"

She waved goodbye at the door and left the suite, a lighter spring in her step than had been there before.

CHAPTER FIVE

"Talk about deja vu," Vera commented when they approached the bar and noticed Frederick talking to yet another woman while Desmond appeared to examine the crown molding with great interest. "They should have called this the Isle of Lust. Why must your brother always be such a Lothario?" The sight of Freddie's head bent intimately towards another woman sent pings of annoyance flitting through Vera's mind, yet as usual, she couldn't say why.

"He has his moments," Rosemary muttered, approaching the men just as Desmond noticed their presence.

"You both look lovely," he said as he turned to face them, his repositioning allowing for an unobstructed view of Frederick's companion.

She was tall, boasted a voluptuous figure not quite svelte enough to be considered currently fashionable, and was at least forty years old by Rosemary's estimation. A handsome looking forty, but forty all the same. Vera noted that the dress she wore was couture, and probably cost a small fortune. On her left hand, a ludicrously large diamond ring flashed even in the dim light of the bar, but she tossed her hair in Frederick's direction anyway.

Even though it felt uncharitable, Rose couldn't help but cast a mark against the obviously spoken-for woman. She couldn't understand the idea of tying oneself to one man if the desire to cat around still lingered, though it seemed to have become a far more frequent occurrence in recent years. Or perhaps, thought Rosemary, she had simply grown up and begun to see things for what they really were.

Sliding her thoughts from her mind and attempting to arrange her expression into something other than contempt, she turned to face Frederick. "Do we have a table?" she asked him.

"Of course, little sister," he replied, a quelling edge to his voice. "But first, meet the lovely Geneviève Chevalier. I expect you two might have a lot to talk about. Geneviève is an artist as well."

She highly doubted she'd find any sort of common ground with Geneviève Chevalier, and her brother knew it. He was simply mischievous, and Rosemary suddenly couldn't wait to find out what form of retaliation Vera would use to put him in his place. If he kept up with his irksome ways, she'd gladly conspire against him on Vera's behalf.

Rosemary held out her hand in greeting but was, instead, pulled into an enthusiastic embrace that left her with a lipstick smear on both cheeks. "Enchanté," Geneviève boomed. "Your charming brother is correct. I sculpt and dabble in charcoal drawings, which Frederick here tells me is your specialty," she said, slipping seamlessly into accented English. "We must sit down and chat."

Geneviève moved on to greet Vera as if she didn't notice the icy glare being cast in her direction. "That's a beautiful engagement ring," was all Vera said, her flat tone making it more of an accusation than a compliment.

"Mais oui," Geneviève trilled. "C'est très beau, n'est-ce pas? Soon, I'll be Geneviève Marlowe. I know, it doesn't have quite the same ring to it, does it? And there he is, my betrothed." Her gaze shifted towards the entrance, eyes twinkling at the sight of her fiancé.

Vera elbowed Rosemary in her side, and Rose worried that if her friend kept it up, she'd end up black and blue by the end of the holiday. "She's French," Rosemary muttered in response. "They're far more exuberant than the British. Perhaps they have some sort of understanding."

Geneviève displayed not a single ounce of shame at her flirtatious behavior, and it soon became apparent that Rosemary had been correct, for it was a trait she shared with the man she intended to marry.

"I see you've made friends, darling," the man said, his gaze landing on Vera and Rosemary. He was the same man from the lift the day before; the one who had rubbed them both the wrong way from the very first word out of his mouth. Rosemary rolled her eyes; it made perfect sense that these two should be paired up.

Geneviève let out a trilling laugh and kissed her fiancé on the lips. "I always do, mon amour. This is Frederick, his friend Desmond and sister Rosemary, and her friend Vera. They've just come from London. Everyone, this is Benjamin Marlowe."

"Please, call me Ben. And, I've already had the pleasure of meeting these two lovely ladies, haven't I?" he said, flashing a smile he clearly considered charming. Instead, Rosemary felt as though she'd brushed against something slimy.

"Yes," Vera murmured, "we've met." Her clipped response should have been enough for Frederick to realize this was not the sort of company the women cared to dine with, but he either didn't notice or intentionally ignored the tension while offering to share a larger table with the couple. Vera and Rosemary sent twin glares at his back while being directed towards their seats.

The table was a rectangular one, with room for two people on each side, and one on each end. Somehow, Geneviève managed to position herself as far away from her fiancé as she could and sat at one of the ends, flanked by Freddie and Desmond. That left Rosemary and Vera trapped on either side of Ben, across from one another. Thinking it best to keep Vera as far away from Frederick as possible, Rosemary sat next to him and resisted the urge to stomp on his toes herself. Every so often, Des would smile apologetically from where he sat, kitty-corner to her.

"It's a lovely hotel, isn't it?" Rosemary directed her comment to the entire table once the waiter had taken their drink order—cocktails, of course, plus a lavishly expensive bottle of Cabernet that Benjamin insisted they all must try.

Geneviève made a noise that might have been a dainty, French-sounding snort, and rolled her eyes. "Eh, zis tells me you are not a seasoned traveler, Rose."

If she was trying to annoy her, Geneviève missed the mark. Rather, her disdain amused Rosemary, who refused to rise to the bait even when the pushy, overly enthusiastic woman called her by a shortened version of her name.

"Ze hotel is like a Monet, is it not?"

"I would have to disagree," Rosemary replied lightly as her agile mind processed the reference. "But then again, I may not have your vast experience from which to draw."

For a moment, Geneviève's lips pursed as she tried to discern whether Rosemary had paid her a compliment or delivered a subtle dig at her age.

Frederick appeared perplexed, prompting Geneviève to explain, "you see, from far away, it's lovely—a full picture, skillfully painted, depicting a scene of great beauty. However, the closer you get, the blurrier it becomes. One can see all the minute flaws, the individual brush strokes. It is, essentially, rather a messy interpretation of a lovely scene."

While Frederick laughed at the analogy, somewhat more uproariously than necessary, Rosemary offered her observations. "I've always felt it is the quality of the viewing eye rather than the art itself that denotes what is pleasing. Monet sought to capture the playful nature of light itself, rather than the hard surface upon which it landed."

Rosemary said her piece with a warm smile, leaving Geneviève again to wonder at the intent behind the comment.

Without clarifying further, Rose continued, "We've enjoyed our stay immensely so far." She didn't mention that it would have been a much better experience had they been given the other suite they'd booked—the one taken by Geneviève and Benjamin. Such criticism would only lend support to the woman's statements, so once again, Rosemary smiled.

Unable to refute such a benign rebuke, if it was such, Geneviève turned her attention back to Frederick, entertaining him with inappropriate tales of her artistic exploits. Were the woman to be believed, she had been the inspiration for a nude portrait that now hung in the Louvre.

Vera noted with some venom that the story had had the desired effect, as Frederick's gaze was practically pinned to the woman's ample bosom. Had she been sitting next to him, Frederick would have been the victim of a purely accidental drink spillage. As it was, she could only express her ire by a somewhat ineffectual stomp of her pointy heel on the tip of his shoe. Hampered by distance, she barely made a dent, and the assault went ignored save for an absently apologetic glance as he pulled his foot back towards his side of the table.

Meanwhile, Benjamin took the opportunity to pelt Rosemary and Vera with his own spate of boasting. "They'll be finished building my new yacht just in time for next year's boating season. It takes quite a lot of work, you know, and you wouldn't believe the expense—" he waxed on, mentioning a ridiculous amount of money, acting as though the ladies ought to find his extravagance impressive. They didn't.

"I'd love to offer my congratulations on your engagement," Vera finally said to cut off the discussion, and Rosemary smiled as she noticed the offer was made only in theory.

"Tell me, how did you two lovebirds meet?" Vera hoped the mention of their impending union might jar at least half of the couple from blatant flirtation, though both would be preferable.

Benjamin winked at his fiancée across the table. "Ah, what a lovely story. I'd just moved from London to Paris. Had some work to do there, investments to make. You see, the French market—" he began to launch into another boastful story but was quickly waylaid by Geneviève.

"Mon cher, they don't want to hear about that. What happened was zis," she said as she leaned towards the group conspiratorially. "I stole him away from another woman."

How that was a *lovely story* was beyond Rosemary's comprehension, but at that point, nothing about the couple would have surprised her.

"True, true, my love," Benjamin said with a grin, "quite a beautiful woman too, but no match for Vivi here. I walked into a little out-of-the-way nightclub in Paris, and there she was at the bar surrounded by a group of adoring men. From the second we locked eyes, I knew I was going to marry her. In fact, I walked up to her and told her just that."

"He did!" Geneviève trilled. "In terrible, broken French, I might add. Why he thought moving to Paris without knowing French was a grand idea, je ne le saurais jamais! And what did I say to you, darling?"

"She said I'd have to show her a copy of my bank statement first! Can you believe the cheek?" Benjamin boomed. "I knew right then I'd met my match. We've been together ever since." He laughed so loudly, nearly everyone in the lounge must have been able to hear him. An older woman at the table nearest theirs sent an annoyed look and a harrumph in his direction.

A tap on his shoulder startled Benjamin, and when he turned, it was to find Walter, the assistant manager, staring down at him. "Sir, would you mind lowering your voice? While we appreciate that you're enjoying yourself, we've had a few complaints from other tables regarding the noise."

Walter seemed more concerned with staring down the front of Geneviève's dress, which did indeed draw the male eye, than he did in reprimanding Benjamin. The woman's wink in his direction did nothing to dissuade him, and in fact, the man appeared as if he might begin to drool at any moment.

"Sure, sure," Ben replied jovially, though he threw a stony look after the assistant manager's retreating back. After that, dinner wrapped up rather quickly, the mood having been extinguished. Desmond hardly said a word during the meal, and everyone save for Frederick, who had been having a grand time, was relieved when the bill came.

"Let me," Benjamin reached for the slip of paper, but his movements seemed slow, and Rosemary noted his assessing gaze darted between her brother and Desmond. When Frederick also reached out, Ben hastily withdrew his hand, leaving Freddie on the hook for the expensive bottle of wine.

"I, for one, am completely exhausted," Vera said with an exaggerated yawn as she rose from the table. Rosemary quickly agreed.

Always the gentleman, Desmond offered himself and Frederick as escorts to the women's' suite. It seemed as though he was as desperate to get away from Geneviève and Benjamin as they were.

"We can all ride the lift up together," Geneviève said, squelching that plan. "I'll need to freshen up before we head to the bar."

"Wonderful," Vera whispered in Rosemary's ear, making her choke back a snort.

"Thank goodness the suite is well-stocked," she whispered back. "I need at least two more cocktails after that dinner."

Outside, the wind whipped hard enough to cause the lights inside the hotel to flicker. Relieved for the excuse, Vera said loud enough for everyone to hear, "It sounds as though it might be rather chilly this evening; hunkering down in the comfort of our suite sounds just lovely."

"Convenez-vous," Geneviève replied lightly. "Suit yourself."

On their way through the lobby, Richard Wright's furious voice commanded attention. His spine ramrod stiff, he banged a hand on the reception counter with one fist, the other he held at his side.

"I still cannot fathom how you've managed to keep this hotel afloat considering the abysmal level of service your guests receive." The man was relentless, and when Cecily stepped out from the office behind the counter, she looked as though she might thoroughly enjoy wringing his neck with her bare hands. She rounded the counter to face him head-on.

His attention switching from Gloria to Cecily, Wright loomed over her to continue his tirade.

From his position near the lift, Benny said, "See here, now." His normally placid expression settled into a frown as he took a few steps towards the angry man.

Cecily's hand came up to warn Benny back. "Mr. Wright, if you're unhappy here," she snapped, "you're more than welcome to try your luck at one of the other hotels on the island. In fact, if you continue to badger the staff, I'll have to insist you procure other lodgings."

Out of nowhere, Geneviève squared her shoulders and strode the rest of the way across the lobby, piercing Cecily with a cold look. "If zis is how you speak to your *guests*—then it's no wonder he's upset. Mon Dieu!" She glared at Cecily and opened her mouth as if she were about to say something else, but Benjamin took her by the arm and led her towards the lift.

"Come on, now, Vivi," he said. "It's time we were on our way." Geneviève let herself be pulled away, and Richard Wright, apparently having lost his steam, followed. When the lift failed to move no matter how many times Benjamin pressed the button, another tirade regarding the state of affairs at the Aphrodite erupted as Mr. Wright clamored up the stairs ahead of the couple.

Rosemary and company lingered near the reception desk to offer Cecily their support after the inappropriate outburst.

"Don't you fret, dears," Cecily said, flashing them a genuine smile. "Mr. Wright blusters, but I know just how to handle him. Gloria," she said in a much softer tone, "you look simply knackered. I'll send for Margaret to come in early and you can take the rest of the night off. That man could try the patience of a saint."

She winked in Rosemary's direction, then turned back to Gloria, who looked surprised. "And Gloria, you can bin any further missives from Mr. Wright." Smiling, Cecily strode off to summon Margaret.

Chapter Six

"Well, that was certainly interesting," Rosemary said with a grin. She'd kicked off her shoes and was settled comfortably in one of the armchairs in the suite's sitting room. Vera had dispensed with the mixers and poured them each a generous glass of gin, which Rosemary sipped appreciatively. "We *were* hoping for some excitement to complement our relaxing holiday, so I suppose we ought to count the redoubtable Vivi Chevalier and her deplorable fiancé as such and consider it a success."

Vera glared at her friend, "how dare you say that? It was like torture sitting there all evening watching her fawn all over your brother." At Rosemary's raised eyebrow, she hastened to add, "she's engaged, and it's simply not right."

"Where did this sudden burst of propriety come from? Do you realize who you sound like? You sound exactly like *me*," Rose said, grinning. "I believe we've experienced a reversal of roles."

"You picked a fine time to broaden your ethical horizons, Rosie."

"It isn't as though I'm advocating her behavior, Vera. It's simply not my problem. Nor yours. She won't get anywhere with Freddie, not really," Rosemary said wryly. "He merely likes to puff out his chest and act the big man. What he really wants is to settle down with a nice girl. Not too nice, mind you. He needs to be thoroughly entertained, and as yet no woman has been able to keep him on his toes. I suspect he'll find someone before long." She watched Vera's face carefully but left the rest of her thoughts unsaid, merrily taking another drink.

Vera flopped into a chair, somehow managing not to spill a drop of gin, and sighed. "I suppose you're right. It's simply that, well, I was hoping for an evening with just the four of us. You know, like old times."

"It's only our second night on the island," Rosemary reassured her. "I'm sure there will be plenty of intimate dinners with just the four of us over the next few weeks. To tell the truth, I'm surprised you feel that way. I assumed you'd be racking up flirting partners far faster than my fool of a brother. From what I've heard, the island doesn't lack for eligibles, or for jazzy nightlife. What exactly is standing in your way?"

With another sigh, Vera threw her head back and stared at the ceiling before answering, "I think I've had enough of men for the time being."

Rosemary nearly spat her drink onto the beautiful Persian rug. "Say that again, please, I want to remind you of it the next time you find yourself besotted by some tall drink of water with fire in his eye."

"I'm restless, I suppose. Men are all the same, deep down. At least the ones who chase me. The men who follow you around have substance; the ones who come after me just see the pomp and circumstance. They never really try to get to know me. They treat me like I'm a piece of fluff, and that's where it ends. Maybe I want more than that."

It was more of an admission than Vera had ever made, and Rosemary felt as though something was coming down the pike for her friend. It was about time, in her opinion.

When the door slid open a crack to admit Anna, Vera burst out in surprise. "Well, where did you come from, then?" She'd have sworn the young maid was already tucked up in bed.

"Sorry, Miss. I didn't mean to disturb you. I was talking to some of the staff and lost track of time." Red-faced, Anna bustled around the suite, putting things to rights. "It won't happen again."

"Nonsense, Anna. You've done nothing wrong, and there's no need to scurry about as though you're breaking curfew. You look better, I must say. The color is returning to your face." In fact, there was a pretty flush to the girl's cheeks, but Rosemary decided not to pry.

How long they stayed up talking, Rosemary couldn't say, but when Vera's eyelids began to droop and she begged off for bed, it must have been close to two o'clock in the morning. Rosemary wandered onto the balcony and noticed someone coming up the path from the beach. Squinting, she made out Mr. Wright's bald head shining in the light of the moon. As she shivered in the cool breeze, she wondered what he'd been doing out and about but didn't linger on the notion, as the insufferable man's schedule was none of her concern.

Rosemary slept restlessly that night, her dreams interrupted by terrible visions. It had been this way since Freddie's unfortunate arrest; during the day, she could control her thoughts, but under the cover of darkness, the horrors she'd seen combined with the pain of losing Andrew manifested in the form of nightmares.

After she had watched the bodies of her friends and family pile up behind her eyelids, she decided she'd had enough and rose from the comfort of her bed to pace around the suite. She opened the terrace door quietly, trying to avoid waking Anna or Vera, and stepped onto the cool flagstones. Amid a swath of pink and gold, the sun rose over the mountains until there was nothing but blue sky as far as the eye could see. The dreadful breeze from the evening before seemed a distant memory.

Deciding that the sand and sparkling water were too inviting to ignore, Rosemary dressed quickly and took the stairs to the first floor. By the time she arrived at the bottom, she regretted having declined the use of the lift. The sheen of sweat on the back of her neck made an early morning swim an even more desirable notion.

A half-loaded maid's cart blocked the door to the reception area, trapping Rosemary in the stairwell. "Hello?" she called and jumped when her question was answered with a bloodcurdling scream.

Charlotte, the maid, stepped out from the storeroom situated down the hallway to the left of the stair landing, her eyes the size of dinner plates and her hair a disheveled mess. She looked as though she hadn't got a wink of sleep the night before and hurried to smooth her wrinkled uniform when she realized who stood in the stairway. "Oh, I'm so sorry, Miss—Miss—" she stammered.

"Rose, it's Rosemary—"

"Miss Rose, I'm so sorry. You startled me. I'm afraid I'm rather easily frightened," Charlotte explained.

"It's all right," Rosemary replied once her heartbeat returned to its normal rhythm. "I just needed to get past your cart." She gestured towards the front reception area, sending Charlotte into another round of apologies. Rosemary suppressed the urge to roll her eyes up towards the heavens and reassured the girl a second time, then was nearly bowled over when someone attempted to shove past her.

"Charlotte, what on earth is going on? Why are you screaming like a banshee?" Gloria admonished. "We have guests, you know."

"It's my fault," Rosemary explained. "I startled her is all."

"Well," Gloria said, looking up and down the hallway, "I'd say you'd better get back to work before her strictness—I mean Miss DeVant—shows up to pin your ears back for you."

If Rosemary hadn't liked Gloria much before, she certainly didn't care for her now after hearing her talk about her superior in such a manner in front of a guest, and particularly after Cecily had been so kind to her the evening before. The red tinge that rose to Gloria's cheeks when she realized the gaffe did little to alleviate Rosemary's irritation.

Rosemary ducked out and Gloria followed, Charlotte's tittering still echoing behind her.

"Drat," she said out loud as she stepped outside onto the flagstone path that led directly to the beach. "I forgot to bring a towel. And now I'm talking to myself." Rosemary wondered if a dip in the sea was worth the trouble of returning to her room, and then realized she didn't have to go that far after all.

48

She retraced her steps to where Charlotte stocked her cart, and this time made sure not to startle her. "I'm looking for a towel," she said gently, frowning when she realized the cart was filled with sheets instead.

"The cupboard on the other side of the stairwell has towels," Charlotte explained and tried to maneuver around the cart that was blocking her into the storeroom. Rosemary now understood why she'd placed it at the bottom of the stairs.

"I can help myself if that's all right," she told the girl, who nodded gratefully.

"Of course, take as many as you need. Reach up, and you'll find the cord for the light."

Rosemary pulled open the door Charlotte had indicated and took a step forward, her arm reaching high for the cord. Her foot knocked into something on her way, and when the light came on, Rose thought for a long, drawn-out second that she was still trapped in one of her nightmares.

There, dead on the floor in a pool of blood, lay the unmistakable figure of Cecily DeVant. Tears sprang to Rosemary's eyes, and her hand fluttered to her mouth, as much in shock as to keep herself from heaving. An ear-piercing scream erupted from her throat.

Out in the hall, Charlotte struggled with the cart but wasn't able to break free before Gloria arrived on the scene, her brows drawn down in consternation.

"For the love of all that is good and holy, Charlotte," she snapped as she rounded the corner, "what on earth—" she broke off her diatribe when she realized it wasn't Charlotte but rather Rosemary screaming, then rushed towards the cupboard door.

"Oh—oh—oh no!" she wailed into the silence left when Rosemary abruptly quieted. "Stay back, Char. Go out to the lobby. Ring for the police."

Later, Rosemary would appreciate the efficiency with which Gloria handled the situation, but right then all she could do was sob. Cecily wasn't the first murder victim she'd ever seen—and it was clear as day that this was indeed murder—but it *was* the first time she'd actually had affection for the body she'd happened upon.

49

"She's dead, isn't she?" Gloria asked, her voice flat and devoid of emotion.

"Yes," Rosemary said after a long pause. "She's most certainly dead." From somewhere deep down, she summoned the strength to examine Cecily not as a friend but as an investigator. She knew the scene would be, as all the others were, permanently seared into her memory, and she wanted to ensure she didn't miss what might turn out to be a vital clue.

Spatters of blood colored the stacks of stark white towels a macabre crimson, which meant the crime had been committed here, in the storeroom. Judging by the angle, Cecily had been kneeling down when she was struck on the back of the head. The only other sign of trauma was a shallow scratch on Cecily's forehead.

Rosemary had already ruled out the possibility that the death had been an accident, but the site of the wound clinched it. That, and the fact that whatever weapon had struck the fatal blow was nowhere to be seen. She looked for blood on the corners of each shelf just to make sure it couldn't have been an unfortunate accident but found none.

Once satisfied, and with a sorrowful glance at Cecily's unusual face, she turned and walked slowly through the door, across the lobby, and into the bathroom where she finally allowed herself to break down. Sobs turned to dry heaves from her empty stomach, and the pounding in her head hammered up a decibel until it was deafening. So deafening she didn't realize someone was pounding on the door.

"Just a minute," Rosemary called, attempting to keep her voice even. She rose and splashed water on her face in a vain attempt at cleaning herself up before opening the door. She had never been so glad to see Vera's face in all her life and allowed herself to be gathered into her friend's outstretched arms.

"Are you all right? That receptionist called up to the suite and told me what happened. Fred and Des are on their way down. I told Anna to stay behind. She doesn't need to be involved in this," Vera said, her voice shaking. She'd wanted to ask straight away what had happened, but since a part of her didn't really want to know, she waited until Rosemary had collected herself.

"You're quite right about Anna," Rosemary agreed. "It's Cecily. She's been killed." It was all she could say, and it was enough.

Vera turned pale. "Oh, no. Murdered?"

"Yes, I'm positive."

"Then, we'll have to take the case, won't we?"

Rosemary sighed. "I highly doubt the local police will appreciate a couple of women butting into their work, regardless of how successful we've been in the past. However, Cecily was my mother's dearest friend—and after meeting her, I've developed a soft spot for her as well. If there's anything we can do, of course, we will. Let's just keep quiet about this. I certainly hope Frederick hasn't been bragging about our involvement in murder investigations."

"I have not as yet been provided with the opportunity to brag overmuch about anything, dear sister," Frederick's voice was low in Rosemary's ear, and she felt his hand wrap protectively over her shoulder. She turned and buried her head in his chest.

"It's Cecily," she said again, wishing it weren't true.

Her brother swallowed hard and cursed but didn't let her go. "I'm sorry, Rosie. Truly. Now, what are we going to do about it?"

"I'm so sorry, too, Rose," Desmond finally spoke from where his arm was wrapped around Vera's shoulders in a similarly comforting fashion. She was already sick of hearing those words but appreciated the effort just the same. "You've suffered quite a shock. Why don't we take you back to your suite?" he suggested gently.

Rose pushed away from Freddie and shook her head. "No, not yet. I'll have to speak to the police, and I want to check on Charlotte."

She wanted to do more than that; she wanted to observe the reactions of the rest of the staff because it seemed to her that one of them would be the most likely culprit. Often, the murderer couldn't help but show up at the scene of the crime, likely from the need to watch the proceedings whether with vile pleasure or in an attempt to allay suspicion. "The girl would have found the body herself if I hadn't been there. I believe the towel cupboard was her next stop."

"You don't think that young little maid could have killed Cecily, do you?" Vera asked in a high-pitched, incredulous tone.

Rosemary shook her head. "No, not really. However, I honestly couldn't say what she's capable of. If she didn't do it, she's suffered quite a shock. Charlotte wasn't the only one of the staff who had reason to resent Cecily's iron fist, that's for certain."

And while Rosemary did suspect that whoever had killed Cecily likely worked at the Aphrodite, she couldn't help but remember the look of sheer loathing on Geneviève's face the night before.

Chapter Seven

Several hours later, Rosemary found herself sitting in what must have been Cecily's office, being grilled by an uptight, quite British policeman by the name of Inspector Boothe.

"Where exactly were you yesterday evening between the hours of ten o'clock and midnight?" he asked Rosemary. She didn't particularly care for the way he spoke to her, as if she were the prime suspect in Cecily's death, but she knew he was only doing his job. She had, after all, found the body, but it was exasperating to know he should have been focusing his attention elsewhere.

Pushing grief aside, Rosemary replied, "I had dinner with my traveling companions and two other guests. Geneviève Chevalier and Benjamin Marlowe. None of us left the group alone, and the waiter can attest to our presence. We finished eating at around nine o'clock, and I went to my suite with my friend, Vera Blackburn, who is staying with me. We had a few drinks but stayed in our room for the rest of the night." She'd answered his next two questions before he could even ask them, which seemed to do less to clear her from suspicion than she'd hoped.

He peered at her from beneath raised eyebrows. Rosemary could tell the expression was habitual, because his forehead

53

remained crinkled even after his features settled back to their normal configuration.

"We'll certainly follow up on that," was all he said before continuing to put her through the third degree. "When was the last time you saw Miss DeVant alive?"

Rosemary was quick to answer, and when she did, there was sorrow in her voice. "She was standing behind the reception desk when we left the restaurant. We had a brief conversation before going to our suite."

"About what, exactly, did you converse?" the inspector asked next, firing more questions before she had a chance to respond. "Did you know the victim personally? I was under the impression you're a tourist only here for a short holiday."

With an effort, Rosemary answered calmly. "I didn't know Cecily well, but she is—was—an old friend of my mother's. She was from London, as I'm sure you're aware, as am I. She was dealing with a difficult guest, Mr. Richard Wright, who insisted upon lodging several complaints. It seems he's notorious for doing so, as we've heard him raise his voice more than once during our short stay."

Boothe made a sound somewhere between a snort and a harrumph. "Quite so, quite so."

"Another guest jumped in to defend Mr. Wright. Geneviève Chevalier made no bones about her poor opinion of Miss DeVant and treated her most disrespectfully." The possibility of another suspect occurred to Rosemary. "You might want to speak to Gloria, who works at the front desk. Cecily called her competence into question in front of guests."

"Not that I owe you any explanation, but I've already spoken to Miss Chevalier and her companion, who state they were together all night."

"I'm sure they were."

The inspector ignored her comment and instead kept pressing. "What did you do after you found Miss DeVant's body?"

At his words, the vision of Cecily on the floor sprang back up behind her eyes. She willed herself not to cry and made sure her voice was even when she replied, "I screamed. I screamed,

54

and that's when Gloria came running. One of the maids, Charlotte is her name, was busy filling her cart from one of the other cupboards." She explained how Gloria had told Charlotte not to come close, and how she'd examined the scene and checked for the murder weapon.

"Just what exactly made you assume murder? After all, her death could have been accidental. Perhaps there wasn't a weapon at all. Perhaps Miss DeVant fell and hit her head on something inside the cupboard." Rose could tell he was trying to get her goat, and it irked.

"Are you saying you think she fell backwards, hit her head hard enough to cause a mortal injury, then closed the door behind herself? Furthermore, I surveyed the area and found nothing that could have caused that type of wound. She was lying on her side, giving me a clear view. I didn't touch the body or anything else, for that matter."

Inspector Boothe raised an eyebrow, "How very convenient."

Rosemary raised her eyebrow in return. "I think *helpful* is the word you're looking for, Inspector." As soon as the words left her lips, Rosemary wished she hadn't uttered them, but something about the man sitting before her made her feel like a child who'd been called to the headmaster's office.

"You may want to censor yourself here in Cyprus, Mrs. Lillywhite. This isn't London, and your insolence won't be tolerated. No matter how many murders you've helped solve back in England. Yes, I've already made inquiries, and according to a Detective Inspector Maximilian Whittington, you're quite the amateur sleuth." There was no question this time, just a statement of the facts that Rosemary couldn't—and wouldn't—refute.

She kept her mouth set in a thin line and bit back an uncharitable word or two. All the while, her stomach fluttered at the mention of Max. Wishing vehemently that he were here instead of the man sitting before her, Rosemary fought the urge to defend herself and failed.

"I have been unfortunate enough to have become involved in two cases, and fortunate enough to have identified the murderer in both instances. I'd say I'm more of an asset than a liability, wouldn't you, Inspector?"

"That remains to be seen," he countered. "For now, you're not to leave the hotel area and certainly not to return to London until all inquiries have been made. You're dismissed," he said as if she were one of his deputies.

With all the dignity she could muster, Rosemary exited the office. Outside the door, she ran into Charlotte, who was pacing restlessly while waiting for her turn to be questioned. She appeared positively petrified, so Rosemary stopped to see if there was anything she could do to help.

"Are you all right, Charlotte?" she asked, placing a comforting hand on the girl's shoulder.

"Yes. I mean, no, of course not. How could I be?" Charlotte said, her eyes ringed with red. "Miss DeVant was…" her voice became thick, and she trailed off. Rose wasn't upset that she didn't finish her sentence; the last thing she wanted to hear was another stab at the dead woman's character. Charlotte continued once she'd collected herself. "She didn't deserve to die like that. Nobody does. And to think, we were all tucked into our beds while it was happening." She shivered at the thought, her gaze not quite meeting Rosemary's eyes as she stared off into the distance.

Rose nodded in agreement, attempting to provide comfort, but all she could think was that clearly, not *everyone* was tucked into their bed during Cecily's murder.

"Char," a girl she'd not yet been introduced to tapped Charlotte on the shoulder. She was dressed in a receptionist's uniform, and wore a fretful expression.

Charlotte jumped, startled again, and bit back a scream. Instead, she caught her breath and pursed her lips at the other girl. "Margaret, you scared the daylights out of me. I'm afraid my nerves are simply shot today."

"I'm sorry, I thought you'd like to know that Gloria said you could be dismissed after you speak to the inspector," Margaret explained. She looked to be about the same age as Charlotte; hardly more than a girl, but with a professional demeanor that suggested she had much more work experience.

Charlotte appeared skeptical. "Really?" she asked. "That's quite nice of her, isn't it? If somewhat out of character." She opened her mouth once more, but shut it abruptly, perhaps to avoid saying something uncharitable about Gloria. It seemed Cecily wasn't the only one who had earned a reputation for being a pill.

Margaret raised an eyebrow, and nodded, "Take the reprieve and be grateful for it. You'll likely never be offered another."

With a nod, Charlotte agreed, "I believe you might be right about that."

Chapter Eight

"That horrid man actually suspects I'm the one who killed Cecily," Rosemary ranted once she'd been reunited with her brother and her friends. They'd taken seats out on the terrace, far away from prying ears, to discuss how to proceed.

"Is that what he said to you?" Desmond boomed, far louder than he'd intended.

"Not in so many words," Rose said, placing a quelling hand on his arm. "But he did command me to not leave the hotel property. I suppose that means we won't be taking your hike in the hills anytime soon."

"To hell with the hike, Rose. This is ludicrous, and I've half a mind to—" Des's voice took on a menacing tone.

"You and me both," Frederick enthusiastically agreed.

"You'll not do anything, my dears. It will all be sorted out in due time. I didn't kill her, and there are far more interesting suspects than me." For some reason, their exuberance took some of the steam out of her own irritation.

Vera sipped her orange juice—sans alcohol, for once—and directed a glare towards the general area of the hotel. "He looked like a bloody bulldog—the inspector, I mean, and I always put stock in first impressions. That means it's up to us to figure out who really did it. For goodness sake, Rosemary. When did you become a magnet for murder?"

"I've been asking myself that very same question since the moment I turned on the cupboard light and saw poor Cecily lying there. It hasn't really sunk in yet that she's dead. She had so much life left in her; so much spunk. I admired her, just as Mother said I would. It's a tragedy is what it is, and I've had just about enough tragedy to last three lifetimes. That inspector can suspect me all he wants. I'll make him look a right fool by the time I'm done." Rosemary sat back, took a swig of the brandy Frederick had placed in front of her, and finally noticed the gaping expressions on her friends' faces.

"What?" she asked.

"Nothing, Rosie," Vera said with a grin, "it's simply been ages since you've worked up a good angry fit. I think you're finally coming out of your funk."

Rosemary didn't think 'funk' was the word she'd use to describe mourning her dead husband, but then Vera had never been one to mince words.

"It's a *good* thing, Rose. We're *all* fired up over this one. Cecily wasn't some gambling kingpin or war profiteer like our last two victims. She was a spitfire of a woman, and we all adored her at first sight. I can't believe whoever did this had a valid reason. It feels petty and tragic. Although I will admit, we didn't know her *that* well."

Frederick grimaced. "No, perhaps not, but I believe you're on the right track. What do you think, Rose?"

"I think our friend had quite a few enemies, and we're going to have to weed through them all if we want to figure out who had it in for her bad enough to kill her. The staff is our first priority. Something about that maid, Charlotte, strikes me as off. Anna thinks so, too. She was on the spot when I found Cecily, but the murder occurred last night, giving her plenty of time to clean up and compose herself. We need to find out more about her, and also Gloria the receptionist. Cecily did, after all, threaten her position. Furthermore, we can't ignore the fact that it could have been any one of the guests. I'm inclined to point the finger at Geneviève Chevalier or that terrible fiancé of hers, Benjamin Marlowe. The way she looked at Cecily last night, it couldn't have only had to do with Richard Wright's complaints."

Vera's eyes lit up. "And what about him? He's been hounding poor Cecily night and day. I heard he's been here for near on a month, and all he *does* is complain. She was in his room yesterday evening, and she was none too thrilled when she left." She explained about how Cecily had come into their suite for a drink. "If you ask me, Wright's the one we should focus on."

"I think Rose is right about this maid," Frederick said, ignoring Vera's comment and causing her to glare at him through slitted lids. He didn't attempt to defend Geneviève or Benjamin, and the oversight probably had more to do with self-preservation than a belief that either of them was involved. For some reason, Freddie always had a soft spot for disreputable characters like the betrothed couple. "Honestly," he continued, still talking about Charlotte. "I've never had such terrible service, even at less reputable establishments. Perhaps she was holding something over Cecily's head, and that's how she's kept her job."

"Cecily ran the tightest ship I've ever seen, so what sort of blackmail could some poor little maid possibly have had on her?" Vera retorted. "And haven't you noticed they're quite understaffed? *That's* probably why she keeps her job." Rosemary and Desmond exchanged a look across the table. Now was not the time for another bout of bickering.

Frederick ignored Vera's defense of Charlotte and snorted, "how should I know what her motive might be? Isn't that what investigations are for? We poke around, figure it out."

"I'm still not convinced," Rosemary interjected. "It would have taken a man—or perhaps a woman in a serious rage—to have committed the crime. I'm not sure that little maid would have been capable of delivering such a blow."

"People have a way of surprising you, Rose," Frederick replied, "especially if they've been pushed close enough to their limit to take another person's life. Add in the effects of a heightened state, and Charlotte could have performed the act. It may be unlikely, but isn't that always the way in the murder mysteries? It's the one you least expect."

When Frederick got his hackles up about something, there was little to be done to deter him. "Why don't the two of you"—

she glanced at Desmond— "follow your own lead then, and we'll follow ours." Her bald statement made Vera's lips lift into a smile.

"That sounds like a lovely idea to me." Vera agreed. "I'd bet a thousand pounds we'll figure out who the murderer is before the two of you do."

"Oh, I'd take that bet," Frederick said, squaring off with her.

Desmond appeared less than impressed with the plan. Considering he had barely said a word, and certainly hadn't agreed with Frederick, the apathy didn't come as much of a surprise to Rosemary. She cast him a pleading look, to which he acquiesced, nodding to indicate he'd act as babysitter for Frederick.

"Then it's settled, but we're not placing bets on who will avenge the death of a woman we admired. It's distasteful," Rosemary reprimanded. "Honestly, the two of you!"

Freddie and Vera had the decency to look chagrined, and they both mumbled an apology, unwilling to risk having Rose's wrath turned upon them.

Chapter Nine

The sea swallowed the last pink and glowing rim of the sun as Rosemary stood on her balcony and watched, her heart heavy with sorrow over Cecily's loss. She'd have to wire her mother and break the bad news, but that was a chore for the next day.

"Since I'm not allowed to leave the premises, why don't we go down to the outdoor bar and let off some steam?" Rosemary suggested. "Perhaps we'll glean some useful information while we're there."

Andrew had always said observation was a detective's most useful tool, particularly when the subjects had no idea one was paying attention. She could almost hear him whispering the words in her ear, but lately, his voice had begun to fade. She wasn't sure anymore whether she remembered it as clearly as she used to, and the thought saddened her.

And so, in her typical fashion, she swept the notion under the rug—pushed it into the deepest corner of her mind where she wouldn't have to think about it until she was alone, back at home, hiding beneath her bed covers.

While she'd been musing, the rest of the group had agreed to her suggestion. They took the lift to the bottom floor, where Vera pulled her across the flagstone terrace and out into the night. Once they'd reached the bottom steps, Vera let go and fell into step beside Frederick, the black silk kimono she'd donned floating prettily on the breeze. Rosemary hardly noticed her friend's ulterior motive and didn't even realize she'd moved away to allow Desmond to take Rose's arm.

She did, however, recognize the subtle signs of being managed, and wished the lot of them would stop treating her as if she were some weak-willed woman who needed constant coddling. What irked was that she couldn't even get mad because she knew it was only out of love for her that they behaved so. Rosemary sighed, resigned herself to her fate, and allowed Des to lead her towards the beachside bar.

As they approached, it became obvious that this was the place where hotel employees came to unwind after a hard day's work. She recognized Gloria immediately, even with her hair done up in some sort of complicated braid rather than hanging around her shoulders as she wore it during working hours.

Margaret the receptionist sat on a barstool just at the edge of the shadows cast from an oil-burning lantern, her eyes shooting daggers towards Gloria every few seconds. Rose wondered if it was professional jealousy or personal, since Gloria sat quite close to Walter, the assistant manager.

Walter must have come straight down after his shift because he still wore the starched shirt and loose pants required of all male staff. He sat on a stool at the corner of the bar where he had the best vantage point to survey the area. From the way he watched the employees through slitted lids, it appeared being truly off the clock was not in his nature.

While neither Charlotte nor Benny were in evidence, she recognized a couple of waiters from the lounge and a floor maid. Richard Wright, the irritable guest, sat alone at a table out of the way. All of them she could stand to be around, but when she noticed Geneviève and Benjamin situated at the other end of the bar, their heads bent conspiratorially, her heart dropped. Rosemary wasn't sure which of the pair was worse, but she had no doubt the two deserved one another.

"Oh, thank goodness," Rosemary said out loud when the couple merely waved and went back to their conversation. "I can't handle her right now. Him either."

Vera opened her mouth to respond and instead sneezed. Once, then twice, a pause, then a third time. "Seconded," she said when her breath returned.

Though Frederick found Vivi delightful, he knew better than to speak out on her behalf, as arguing with his sister never ended well for him. Instead, he found a place at the bar with enough room for all four of them and settled onto a stool.

"Barkeep!" Frederick shouted over the din. "A round of something rummy for my friends. Anything with a nice kick will do."

Rosemary's spot near Walter's back allowed for her to listen in on his conversation with Gloria, and she did so without the usual niggle of remorse at eavesdropping. It helped that the man spoke in louder tones than necessary most of the time.

"Damn shame about Miss DeVant. Can't help thinking if only we'd gone back a little earlier, I might have been able to put a stop to it all and saved that wonderful woman." To Rose's trained ear, Walter's wistful regret struck a false note.

"You couldn't have known, and there's no good that can come of fretting. It's over now, and you're not to blame for spending an hour or two in more entertaining pursuits." Gloria very nearly purred, leaving Rose to assume that she might offer herself as the reward at the end of Walter's quest for fun.

"I suppose you're right. Who do you think killed her? One of the staff maybe? Or a guest?"

"You know that Ben fellow was in a right state last night. Certainly strikes me odd, that one. Not at all a stable chap. Could be something to it, don't you think?" Walter said.

"Yes, I think you might be right," Gloria replied, the breathy note dropping from her tone as Walter seemed not to sense her romantic undertones. "Could be he had another violent episode."

Could be," he mused. Walter lowered his voice, "On the bright side, being the assistant manager and all, I'll probably be tapped to take over in her stead." He sounded rather proud of himself, and Rosemary's head filled with steam.

"Perhaps. Although I wouldn't go on about it too much, if I were you. Might be considered a motive for bumping off the old girl," Gloria said vaguely, sounding suddenly distracted.

"If a chance at running the hotel is a motive, then it's one we share equally. The only reason I was promoted ahead of you is that the bloody dragon didn't like you as—" Walter's comment trailed off.

When Rosemary looked up at Desmond and saw that his cheeks were pink, then glanced back at Gloria, it became clear just what—or rather who—had distracted the woman mid-conversation. Her stomach lurched as she watched Gloria try to get his attention with a little smile here, and a flutter of lashes there. It settled some when she noticed Desmond carefully avoided Gloria's gaze, but then churned some more at the thought of Cecily. The poor woman had been murdered, and all anyone cared about was the state of their jobs—and their loins.

Des caught Rosemary's eye; a flare of hope flickered to life inside him when he saw the irritation on her face. He then did his best to extinguish it. Pressing the issue would only make things awkward between them, as he was sure Rosemary wasn't ready for anything more than friendship.

For the first time since he'd come back into her life, Rosemary considered whether Desmond harbored romantic notions towards her. *Don't be silly*, she told herself as she fiddled with the beads around her neck, *of course he does. You'd have to be quite daft not to notice the signs.* For the first time, she found the idea intriguing rather than alarming.

She shifted her attention back to the situation at hand. Poor Walter realized the situation he was in long after Rose had, and when he did, she watched his face turn stormy. So stormy, in fact, that the hairs on the back of her arms stood on end. When Margaret approached him, a hopeful expression on her face, he barely even glanced at her, his eyes focused elsewhere.

From under the brim of her white straw cloche, Rose watched Gloria lean over and nip the olive from Desmond's martini. With her eyes on his, she closed her teeth over the olive, using them to slide it from the toothpick slowly, her eyes never leaving his.

When Desmond's body stiffened, Rosemary pressed her lips together to hold back a giggle, but she also elbowed Vera in the ribs, happy to, for once, be the one making the jab instead of receiving it.

To her credit, Vera didn't let out an exclamation but merely turned around with wide eyes to see what it was her friend was so eager for her to witness.

"Oh, how very interesting," Vera murmured, now fully intrigued. "Shall we wager on whether Gloria makes any headway there?"

"She's rather an attractive woman." Rosemary's answer wasn't an answer at all.

Vera agreed. "In a florid, obvious way. Not at all the type our Desmond goes for."

A moment later, Desmond proved Vera right by gently rebuffing Gloria's advances and turning away.

"I've had quite enough," Rosemary said when Frederick attempted to press another gin and tonic into her hand. She had to admit, however, that the alcohol had drowned out the horror of the day, made it almost bearable. "I think I'd fancy a walk down the beach, though."

"I'll go with you," Desmond offered, exchanging a look with Freddie, who took a step back and held up his hands in surrender.

"Take care of my sister," was all he said. Vera winked at Freddie and smiled as it suited her unspoken master plan for Desmond and Rosemary.

"Do be a dear, Freddie, and buy me another drink." To Rose, she said, "You run along now, I'll stay behind and keep an eye on your brother. Someone needs to keep him in line."

Chapter Ten

Off down the beach, Rosemary went with Desmond and, once the sounds of revelry could no longer be heard above the roar of the water against the shore, she stopped and took a deep breath. "It smells amazing out here, doesn't it?" she said, as much to him as to herself.

He closed his eyes and took a deep breath through his nose, inhaling not the scent of the sea, but the scent of Rosemary. "It certainly does."

"It's enough to make me dread returning to London." Desmond made no response other than a hum of agreement. "Are you settling down there, or had you planned to move on? It sounded as though you enjoyed traveling around with your great aunt. Did you get a taste of wanderlust?" she wanted to know.

"Sure, I had a grand time," he said, moving a little closer to Rosemary until his arm brushed against hers. "But London has its own draw. My friends are there. You're there." All intention of keeping his feelings to himself had evaporated in a rum-soaked haze.

Rosemary didn't quite know what to say to that, but she felt those blasted butterflies in her stomach take flight and settle into her throat. She swallowed, gathered her considerable courage, and looked him square in the eyes. What she saw there was a smoldering flame, ready to erupt; all she had to do was tilt her head and lower her lashes.

A war raged between Rosemary's heart and her mind. She knew Andrew was gone; he wasn't coming back and he would never begrudge her the chance to be happy, to find love with someone else. Over the past year, she'd examined their relationship through the luxury of hindsight, but not with perfect vision. Instead, she found she'd been looking through rose-colored glasses. No, she and Andrew hadn't been the sort of couple who fought or even disagreed often, and he'd rarely raised his voice to her, but there were still those bumps in the road that every marriage must weather.

For the first time, it didn't feel like a betrayal to admit that, and so she inclined her head, closed her eyes, and waited.

Desmond didn't give the invitation a second thought. He didn't need to know why Rosemary had decided to succumb to the tension that had existed between them since he'd come back into her life. When his lips finally met hers, their touch was tender; the kind of kiss she'd imagined as a girl before she'd known to expect passion rather than sweetness.

Breath meeting breath sent a shiver up her spine, but when the two finally parted, she let out an uncontrollable giggle.

"It really doesn't stroke a man's ego when a woman he kisses laughs in his face," Desmond said wryly.

"No," Rosemary gasped, "I'm not laughing at you. It was a great kiss. Amazing even, just as I'd imagined it."

Desmond blinked. "Just how often have you imagined kissing me?"

"Every night for years, Des dear. I followed you and Freddie around like a little lost puppy when we were children. You must have known I had a hopeless crush on you." How he might not have noticed was a mystery to her.

He shrugged. "We were children, and I found you charming even then. *You* must have known that."

She thought about that for a moment, wondered if, had either of them been daring enough, they might have had an entirely different life. "I didn't," was all she could think of to say.

"It's funny how things turn out, but I'd hope not so funny as to make you laugh at my best attempt," he replied, still confused by her reaction to his kiss.

"I wasn't laughing at your romantic prowess if that's what you're thinking. It's just, well, I hate to bring it up, but I haven't kissed a man other than Andrew in years. I'd been dreading it, if I'm honest, thinking it would be the most painful part of moving on."

She looked up and into Desmond's eyes and saw that he was trying to understand but still appeared puzzled. "It wasn't. Painful, I mean. Just nice. Maybe I'm not explaining it well, but I feel relieved. And lighter, somehow. Thank you."

"You're welcome, I guess," Desmond said. *Thank you* wasn't exactly what a man wanted to hear, but it beat a slap in the face. He'd consider it a win and leave it at that.

Rosemary's heart did feel significantly lighter upon her return to the bar and her friends. She sidestepped Desmond's attempt to grab her hand on the way back across the beach, for somehow, even though she'd allowed him to kiss her, holding his hand felt even more intimate than having his lips on hers.

She was surprised when neither Frederick nor Vera even glanced in their direction. She'd expected some childish snickering at the minimum, and at least one eyebrow wiggle between the two. Instead, their eyes were fixed on something across the way, on the opposite side of the hut.

"Things are about to get interesting, Rosie," Vera said without even looking at her. "Those two are getting heated."

With a glance in Geneviève and Benjamin's direction, Rosemary sighed. The trip to Cyprus suddenly felt like a misadventure. Not only had she become embroiled in an unintended romance and a depressing murder investigation, but she had also now been reduced to an eavesdropping busybody. What she really wanted to do was nab Vera, retire to their suite, and tell her all about what had just taken place on the beach. Those hopes were fated to be dashed, as there would be no pulling Vera away when a knock-down, drag-out fight appeared poised to occur.

"That's enough, Vivi, you're making a scene," Benjamin bellowed, causing everyone who hadn't been watching with avid interest to glance in his direction.

"*I'm* the one making the scene?" Geneviève snapped back. "You're the one yelling at the top of your lungs!" Her voice rose to an octave higher than his, drawing even more attention, and then lapsed into what sounded like French profanity.

Benjamin's face grew redder until it looked as though his head might explode, and he was forced to shout, "You know I can only understand half of what you're saying."

"I'm saying," Geneviève said, switching back to English with an effort, "that you're nothing but a lying, philandering git, and I wish I'd never laid eyes on you!"

Snapping back into work mode, Walter stepped into the fray. "Here now, get hold of yourselves. You're creating a scene."

Quite often, the brave man who places himself between two spitting animals finds himself the new target of their ire. This was the case with Walter. For just long enough to announce that they'd take themselves off if they weren't wanted, Ben and his Vivi joined forces. A detente that lasted mere moments as they moved away from the bar and the fight began again more loudly than ever.

Without a word said between them, Rosemary and her companions rose to follow as a group. Not too close, but close enough to hear Ben and Geneviève going at each other with renewed fervor.

"How dare you to accuse me of ill behavior when you've been out at all hours of the night, eh? I spend half my time alone while you're, qu'est-ce que c'est, catting around."

"You know it wasn't like that."

"Why? Because you say so?" Geneviève let out a loud snort. "Your word is worth nothing. You say you will go and do what needs to be done, but that is a lie. You say you will return in an hour, and it is nearly daybreak before you crawl into bed. "You are a vile thing." her voice dripped with loathing.

"You are a shrew. A harpy." Ben matched her tone with similar venom, prompting Geneviève to tell him in great detail

70

what method she'd employ to take his life should he repeat such
perfidy.

CHAPTER ELEVEN

Vera slept with her arm around Rosemary that night, and she slept lightly knowing the nightmares that had plagued her friend would only increase in frequency after this latest brush with murder. Rosemary woke early with Vera's hand still resting on her shoulder, and it made her feel better to know she had someone in her life who cared as much as Vera did.

The events of the previous day and evening came thundering back; the horror of the morning, finding Cecily's body, and then the sublime sweetness of a long-awaited kiss to end the day. Too many emotions crowded her mind until finally, she decided she wouldn't get any more sleep no matter how long she lay in bed, unable to quell her worries.

Quiet as a mouse, Rose slipped from beneath the covers, dressed quickly, and carefully closed the door behind her. Then, she tiptoed around the sitting room, treading carefully so as not to wake Anna, who slumbered in the next room. Halfway there, her foot caught against the edge of one of the end tables and she cried out, the noise jarring Anna from sleep. The girl bolted out of her room in a panic.

"What is it? It's not another...*murder,* is it?" Anna whispered the word as if saying it too loudly would make it true.

"No, dear, I simply can't sleep and thought I'd go down for an early breakfast. Though now that you mention it, the last time

I went down early wasn't particularly pleasant. I'm sorry to have awakened you. Would you like to join me, or are you able to fall back asleep?"

Anna shook her head. "I'm awake, and I'm starved." The girl looked like she'd barely shut her eyes to begin with, but Rosemary didn't argue or pry. What Anna did on her own time was her own business, and there was enough to worry about already.

After Anna dressed, the two women took the lift to the lobby, where the smells of breakfast made Rosemary's stomach rumble. "It's quite a different atmosphere than it was yesterday, isn't it?" she mused.

"Yes, Miss, something feels rather off, doesn't it? Though I suppose that's to be expected," Anna replied, looking around.

"Certainly," Rose murmured as she surveyed the room. She had no idea who would have been put in charge in Cecily's stead, despite Walter and Gloria's musings, and vehemently hoped it was neither of them. Whoever it was seemed to have instructed the staff to act as though their manager hadn't been bludgeoned to death the day before, but the pasted-on smiles couldn't quite cover the maudlin mood roiling beneath the surface.

Anna nearly tripped over a case that had been placed haphazardly in front of the reception desk, and it took a strong arm from Rosemary to keep the girl from toppling over. Margaret, stationed behind the desk, started.

"Oh, blimey!" Anna said as she righted herself. "What on earth?"

"Miss, I'm so sorry," Benny's voice came from around the corner of the half-loaded cart and was full of contrition. When he came into view, Rosemary noticed his eyes were red and his face carried blotchy shadows. She bit back the sharp reprimand that flirted with the tip of her tongue.

"Benny, you simply must be more careful." Margaret spoke the words Rosemary hadn't had the heart to say.

Benny shot her a contrite look and continued to prattle apologies. Rose let him do so until he ran out of steam and fell silent.

"Are you all right?" she asked, feeling silly for even asking when it was clear he wasn't.

Benny's lip trembled in time with his hands. "Course not. I know it was you who found her. Know you saw what that monster did to her. To poor Miss DeVant."

Rose wanted to reach out and comfort him in some small way, but it wouldn't have been appropriate, and so she didn't. "I didn't realize you two were close," she said instead. "It doesn't seem as though she was well-liked around here." If she was going to be handed a rod and a lure, she wasn't going to turn down the opportunity to fish for information.

"Wasn't," he said matter-of-factly. "But we got on better than most. All Miss DeVant wanted was for us all to represent the Aphrodite to the highest standard." The statement sounded out of character for Benny, but exactly like something Cecily would have said. At least one of her employees had taken her expectations to heart. Margaret listened with veiled interest, but Rosemary saw her mouth quirk at Benny's rehearsed comment.

His eyes widened as though some thought had just occurred to him for the first time. "You don't think it could have been one of us who killed her, do you?"

Rosemary was at a loss as to how to answer the question. On the one hand, Benny seemed harmless and in real distress over Cecily's death. On the other, she couldn't help but hear Gloria's words from the night before; *Ben was in quite a state. Could be he had another violent episode.* Either way, it wouldn't do to sound any alarm bells, and she wasn't sure she could trust him to be discreet.

"I wouldn't know," was all she decided to say on the subject. "But I do know you're right about whoever did this being a monster." She searched his face for any indication that beneath the gentle exterior lay a person capable of murder. "We have to trust that the police will figure it out, and at the very least, the killer will get what he or she deserves."

"They're going to ask us all questions, aren't they?" he asked, turning pale. "I got nothing to tell them, I don't. Was in my cabin all night. In my cabin," he repeated. "You think they'll make me go to the police station?"

"I doubt it," Rosemary assured him. "If they haven't asked to speak to you yet, they likely won't, and if they do, I expect they'll do it here, at the hotel."

The thought seemed to cheer Benny somewhat, and he thanked Rosemary but said he had to get back to work.

"Odd duck, that one," Anna said once he'd taken his leave.

"You aren't kidding." The comment came from Margaret, who began to lean towards Rosemary conspiratorially. Before she could say more, Richard Wright approached the counter and captured her attention with his latest bout of complaints.

"That maid of yours is entirely incompetent. You should see the state of my room, and nobody has been by to fix the squeaky door I told you about two days ago." He appeared to have more to say, but Margaret interrupted him.

"We've had a bit of trouble here, Mr. Wright, as I'm sure you're aware. Your squeaky door hasn't been tops on our list of priorities, as again, I'm sure you can understand." Her tone was far harsher than she might have dared two days earlier with Cecily peeking around corners and assessing the hospitality of her staff.

"Yes, yes, it's a tragedy." He stroked his chin, looking for all the world as if he couldn't care one bit. "However, the world doesn't stop turning, and your business doesn't stop running. In fact, it's all the more reason to invite the owner of this establishment to consider my client's offer to buy him out. After all, if service continues to go downhill, as I expect it will even further now that Miss DeVant is no longer at the helm, they'll have to sell eventually and at a much lower price."

And there it was, his ulterior motive. Rosemary had known the complaints were pointless—a means to an end. She'd seen this kind of estate con before, some old case of Andrew's she didn't have time to dredge from her memory, but Richard Wright ticked all the boxes. He was smarmy, he had his sights set on a bigger prize, and he didn't appear to have a scruple to call his own.

In Rosemary's book, that made him a suspect in her murder. Get Cecily out of the way in a manner bound to create a scandal and leave the hotel ripe for the taking. At least, in Wright's mind.

She doubted Cecily's uncle would kowtow to that kind of pressure, but what did she know about him? Enough to know he'd not only trusted a woman to run his hotel but kept it in the family by putting her in charge, which eased some of Rose's concerns. She wasn't sure why it mattered to her, but she suspected it was because the Aphrodite had mattered to Cecily, and Cecily had mattered to her mother. She didn't want to see the place sold to the highest bidder, and she certainly didn't want to see Richard Wright get away with murder.

"Oh, blimey!" Rosemary said suddenly, in an echo of Anna's earlier exclamation. The maid's wide eyes turned on her mistress who normally spoke more circumspectly. "What is it, Miss Rose?"

"Mother. I meant to send news of Cecily's death today. She'll be crushed, and when she does find out, I won't be there to comfort her."

"No, you'll be here, solving the crime of her dear friend's death," Anna said in a soothing voice. "It's worth more, Miss, as I'm sure Mrs. Woolridge would agree."

Rosemary considered that. "Yes, you're probably right, but I'm just sick about it...I meant to see about sending her a telegram, but then the Inspector confined me to the hotel." She trailed off, and then realized her concern was unwarranted. "They've contacted Max. I trust he's informed Mother, and I suspect *I'll* be receiving a telegram before too long, begging me to return to London." She sighed. "I'll deal with that later. For now, let's get something to eat. Perhaps by the time we're done, the rest of the layabouts we're traveling with will have woken up."

"Perhaps," Anna said, but she sounded doubtful, and when she headed towards the table her mistress normally chose, she was surprised when Rose forcefully directed her towards another, less central selection. One far away from the three old biddies who seemed to pop up at every turn.

"I'm sorry, Anna, but I cannot bring myself to listen to another argument over knitting patterns or weights of worsted right now. Nor can I bother myself to discuss Vera in all her glory while she lies snoring upstairs. We'll sit over in the corner, shall we?"

"By all means, Miss."

They ate in companionable silence, observing the whirl of activity around them. The hotel seemed to attract a particular brand of clientele—none of it local. Hardly anyone appeared to be visiting Cyprus for business reasons, excepting Mr. Wright, as Rosemary had just learned. Most seemed intent on pleasure and jazz of an evening. While the beach seemed teemed with children, there were few in the lounge at such an early hour. Instead, couples dotted the room, leaning over tables and staring into one another's eyes. It was enough to make Rosemary want to sick up.

"Why don't we go check on Vera?" Anna suggested, her eyes on something across the room. When Rosemary turned to look, it was to discover that Walter, who leaned against the reception desk talking to Margaret, was the one bringing a blush to Anna's face.

"Yes, let's," Rosemary agreed, her eyes narrowing speculatively. Her gaze turned to Anna and stayed there until the pair was safely in the lift. Benny closed the door with a "hello again, Misses," and cranked the lever. He appeared to be feeling marginally better than he had earlier but didn't make conversation as they ascended to their floor.

As the lift door opened, so did Benjamin and Geneviève's suite door. Charlotte, her eyes filled with tears, slipped out, holding her right wrist with some delicacy.

"Are you all right?" Rosemary asked, attempting to catch the girl's arm as she hurried past. It seemed she'd asked that question more times lately than she could count.

Charlotte blinked, wouldn't meet her gaze, and said, "Yes, Miss, I'm fine. Simply banged my wrist on one of the end tables. Benny, can you take me downstairs?" she asked and stepped into the lift.

"Course," Rose heard Benny say as he closed the door.

Anna appeared somewhat concerned but shrugged and had turned towards their suite door when Benjamin himself came out of his room with a stormy expression on his face. He didn't stop to make advances on Rosemary or even say hello; barely even glanced in her direction before whipping into the stairwell and descending loudly.

"What do you suppose that was all about?" Rosemary asked.

"She probably did a horrendous job on his room this morning," Anna replied. "She's terribly green, you know. She's hardly been here a month. I'm not sure how she managed to secure the position in the first place, an upscale establishment like this." It was so similar to Frederick's comment regarding his suspicions of Charlotte that it gave Rose a start.

"I asked her where she'd been employed before coming to Cyprus, and she was awfully dodgy about it," Anna continued. Rose absorbed the information, all the while vowing not to discount Charlotte as a suspect, and also not to let Freddie know his theory might actually hold water.

Chapter Twelve

Vera was just beginning to stir when Anna and her mistress reentered the suite. Rosemary jumped onto the bed to rouse her friend, a returned favor for all of the times she had been on the receiving end of such a display.

"Get up, get up, get up," Rosemary chanted at her friend, receiving a cold look from Vera as she sat up and tried to smooth down her disheveled hair.

"What exactly have I ever done to you, besides be a good friend?" Vera asked with a glare.

"Just get up," Rosemary said and walked back into the sitting room. She could hear Vera grumbling while she readied herself.

The sun had risen, bright and hot, begging for the people of Cyprus to come and lounge on sandy beaches or dip their toes in the clear, cerulean water. It would have been easy for Rosemary to allow herself to descend into a maudlin mood, despite the breathtaking surroundings. She was broken up about what had happened to Cecily, but she knew she had to keep her spirits up if she wanted to exact justice on whoever had killed her mother's dear friend. And so, she instructed Anna to pack her and Vera's beach things.

"Anna, where is my sun hat?" she asked after scouring the wardrobe and coming up empty-handed.

Always with an answer to that type of question at the ready, Anna pointed to a low bureau situated along one wall of the sitting room. "I thought that the best place to keep all the things most easily forgotten."

Rosemary opened the top drawer, and sure enough, there was the missing hat. She removed it and began to shut the drawer when she noticed something else laying at the bottom.

"Anna," she said as she picked up a familiar-looking envelope clutch. She racked her brain for where she'd seen it before, and then suddenly remembered that Cecily had brought it into the suite with her the afternoon she died. "How did this end up in here?"

"Oh," Anna explained, "I'd forgotten. I found that on one of the end tables the other day. I didn't recognize it as either of yours. Did you buy it here on the island?"

Rosemary shook her head. "No, it belonged to Cecily. She left it there the evening...well, the evening she died."

Anna watched as Rosemary chewed her lip while attempting to make a decision. "I don't think Miss DeVant would mind if you looked inside," she said quietly.

Rose sighed. "Yes, you're probably right, Anna, and unfortunately, she isn't here any longer to have an opinion on the subject." With a shake of her head she opened the thin purse and pulled out a sheaf of papers. Letters, to be more precise, as she realized what she was holding.

"Oh, no," Rosemary said as she began to read.

Vera poked her head out of the bedroom door, "What on earth is going on?" she asked.

"We found Cecily's handbag, and it's filled to the brim with threatening letters. *You underestimated me, but I know things about you. Give me what I want or else.* That sort of thing," Rosemary explained, her eyes still on the pages.

"Let me see," Vera said, coming to look over Rosemary's shoulder. "They're typed, which means you won't be able to work your magic on the handwriting." As an artist, Rosemary had a knack for such things, but Vera was wrong. That skill could still help her this time. Just as the hand fell into a rhythm with writing to create similar loops and whorls, a typist used patterns in

80

tapping the keys, so that some letters might be darker than the rest. Moreover, with consistent use, worn strikers might jig to the left or right, to create a unique signature.

"Whoever wrote these was smart, I'll give them that. There are no envelopes either. No return address," Rosemary noted. "No way to tell where they came from."

Vera grimaced but then brightened. "They do, however, seem to clarify the motive for her murder. Obviously, it was about blackmail," Vera said proudly, though her grin quickly turned into a scowl. "Drat, that's a point in your brother's favor."

Rosemary wasn't sure she fully agreed. "Perhaps. Love certainly doesn't seem to have anything to do with it. Revenge, possibly, but I rather think you're right. Someone wanted money, or perhaps leverage."

"You don't think Freddie's cockamamie idea about Charlotte having something on Cecily could actually be right?" Vera exclaimed.

Considering, Rosemary shook her head, "No, not really. She's new, she's inexperienced, and yet somehow, she managed to find enough evidence against Cecily to warrant a threat of this nature? Only to keep a job for which she clearly isn't suited?" Rose waved the letters around. "I don't think so."

"Besides, she certainly doesn't have enough clout to follow through if the threats didn't goad Cecily into giving in to the demands. There's only one person I can think of who fits the bill: Richard Wright."

After handing the rest of the letters to Vera to read, Rose settled on the settee, all thoughts of the beach having flown for the moment. When Vera joined her, Rose passed the letters over, then pressed her fingers over her mouth while she thought through everything she knew about the man. She compared him to some of the bad actors she had run across while working cases with Andrew. The more she thought, the more he seemed to fit the profile.

"This has him written all over it. He's in the hotel, so he could have slipped these letters under Cecily's door. It explains why there's no return address. He's obviously invested a lot of time into whatever scam it is he's running here if he's been here

81

as long as Cecily said he has. Maybe he was getting anxious, worrying it might have all been for nothing."

Vera practically tossed herself down next to Rosemary and continued to scan through the letters with a frown marring her pretty features. "What kind of scam do you suspect him of running?"

"Get them to sell at a low price, then flip it to another buyer, perhaps," Rosemary postulated. "There's money to be made here; scads of it. Whatever his end game is, it has something to do with getting his hands on this property."

"It does seem to add up, but we'll need proof. The typewriter! Unless he sneaked into the office to write those letters, right under Cecily's nose, it would have to be in his room. But how would we get in there..." Vera had taken Rosemary's suggestion with gusto, and now was off and running with it.

Her heart pumping at the thought of nailing Richard Wright to the wall, Rosemary began to pace. "We could sneak the key out of the office and check. It wouldn't take much. A couple of distractions, perhaps. You're always a champ when it comes to that. Fancy a reconnaissance trip downstairs?"

Vera gestured to her disheveled appearance. "Sure, just let me make myself presentable." She hurried into the bathroom while Rosemary continued to sift through the letters.

"Should we tell Freddie and Des what we're up to?" Vera's voice carried from the other room.

At the mention of Desmond, Rosemary realized she'd committed the number one best friend gaffe. "No," she answered definitively. "Things are somewhat awkward right now after he kissed me last night." She let the statement fall out of her mouth casually and waited for the fallout.

Vera's face appeared in the doorway, half her hair combed and her eyes the size of golf balls. "Excuse me? Desmond kissed you? Well, the old boy has more guts than I gave him credit for. How was it? *When* was it? Why didn't you tell me before?" The questions flew at Rosemary like shrapnel.

"Which do you want to know first?" she asked, winking at Anna, who was just as avid with curiosity but too polite to question her mistress the way Vera had.

All she received in response was a glare as Vera stood there, arms akimbo, in the doorway.

"All right, all right. It was last night on the beach, during our walk. It was…nice. Normal, really," Rosemary explained.

"Sounds hot, Rosie," Vera replied sarcastically.

Rosemary sighed. "It was sweet. Not exactly passion-filled, but nice, and likely the best widow's first kiss one could have asked for."

"I feel a *however* coming on," Vera said with an eyebrow raise.

"No, not exactly. Well, maybe you're right."

"Of course, I'm right."

"Of course, you are." Rosemary returned the eyebrow raise. "I don't know what the *however* is, that's why a little break from seeing him might do me some good. And, it will keep you and Freddie from bickering, which in and of itself is a good thing. Hurry up now, we can dissect my love life later."

When Vera was ready, they prepared a plan. "Anna, are you in?" Rosemary asked. "You don't have to do this if you don't want to."

"No," Anna said with conviction. "If there's a way I can help, I will." It was settled, and the threesome descended to the first floor via the stairway rather than the lift, which appeared to, once again, be out of order. When they were at the bottom, Rosemary raised herself up on her tiptoes and peered out the little window that looked onto the lobby.

"Gloria must be off this afternoon. Margaret is still manning the reception counter."

"Good," Vera replied, "she'll be an easier target." Her shoulders squared, she strode out of the stairwell and approached the desk. Rosemary and Anna followed, pretending to have urgent business with the brochure stand near the entrance door, and waited.

"I seem to be having a problem with my room key," they overheard Vera explaining. "And I simply must get back inside quickly." Poor Margaret tried to insist upon sending up the porter, but Vera pressed the issue until the girl sighed, retreated into the office for a moment, and then accompanied her to the stairs.

Anna muttered under her breath. "I wish I had half of Vera's powers of persuasion."

"There doesn't seem to be much she can't wheedle out of a person, does there?" Rosemary agreed. "Now, you stand watch and give the signal if anyone approaches the office door." Putting her trust in Anna, she looked surreptitiously around and slipped inside. It being just on teatime, the place was deserted and the office empty.

What she found, Rosemary hadn't expected. Cecily had been a stickler for procedure, and it made sense that her office would have been ruthlessly organized. Except now, there were file folders and papers stacked high on every surface; drawers had been overturned and rifled through. She knew from experience the police didn't often care whether they made a mess, and suspected they'd thoroughly searched the office for any clue as to who might have killed Cecily.

She reached for where the keys were hung, and her hand hovered over the one labeled with Richard Wright's room number while she wrestled with what she was about to do. Too late to change her mind now, she grabbed the key and pocketed it. With a peek out the door to ensure nobody was coming, Rosemary took the opportunity to poke around. Her eyes landed on a cabinet marked "employee files," and she quickly crossed the space to take a look.

Just as she opened the top drawer, she heard Anna's signal and grabbed the first file she could get her hands on. It was labeled with Benny's full name, and since there was little time for dalliance, she shoved it beneath her blouse and tiptoed back out of the office and around the corner to where Anna was stationed just as Margaret returned to her post.

An irritated looking Benjamin Marlowe marched into the lobby and passed by where she and Anna were huddled. He didn't look up but made a beeline for the lift. "Let's wait, I am in no mood to ride up to our floor with that man," Rosemary said, receiving a nod of agreement from Anna.

Charlotte emerged from the stairwell just as Benjamin Marlowe realized the lift was out of order. He appeared to be in quite a hurry and started when she bustled out in front of him. Rose couldn't see Charlotte's face, her view obstructed by Benjamin, but she saw the girl quail when she nearly bumped into him.

She also couldn't hear their conversation, though by the way he cocked his head to one side while speaking to Charlotte, Rosemary guessed he was having a go at her the same way he had with Vera.

"Interesting," she murmured to herself. "Particularly after seeing her come out of his room in tears just this morning."

"He has positively no decorum, does he?" Anna replied in a shrewd assumption of the situation. It wasn't the first time a similar comment had been made about Benjamin Marlowe.

Rosemary shook her head. "None that I can see. What could Geneviève possibly be thinking by agreeing to marry a man like that?"

"Some women simply don't care whether their husbands are faithful, as long as they're taken care of in the manner to which they've already become accustomed. Unfortunately for Ben, I don't believe he has two pence of his own to rub together."

"What makes you say that?" Rosemary wanted to know.

Anna grinned, and there was an uncharitable glint in her eye. "I saw him stealing toiletries off one of the maid's carts. Why would one need to steal soap if he had money to spare?"

"A very good question, Anna."

Benny's file, Rosemary found quite disappointing, as it consisted of little more than the address and a recommendation from his former employer. According to the short missive, Benny was a good and conscientious worker who required more training than average to understand his duties.

"According to one Aloysius Highbrown, Benny is a loyal soul, but slightly slow to learn." It all added up to what Rosemary had observed since her arrival. "I see no mention of violence, nor of any untoward incident whatsoever."

"Could be this Highbrown fellow was eager to pawn his problems off onto Cecily," Vera offered a possibility.

85

"Hmm, you could be right. Besides, I lean towards Mr. Wright as the more valid suspect. I shall be very interested to see what we find in his room."

Except that the pursuit of illicit information would have to wait, for Mr. Wright, without knowing how his actions annoyed them, remained entrenched in his room the entire day, leaving the intrepid sleuths no opportunity to snoop. A situation Vera found highly amusing for a time, but eventually she became bored to the point where she forced Rose to abandon all hope and try the next day again.

"This is, after all," she insisted, "a holiday. Cecily would want us to enjoy ourselves to the extent that we can."

Whether or not that was true, Rose allowed herself to be carted off to the beach where Vera attempted to bake away her sniffles.

Chapter Thirteen

Cecily's body would be shipped back to England, and the scheduled day dawned bright and sunny, just as every other day on the island had. The atmosphere dismayed Rosemary, who felt the drear and drizzle of London more appropriate weather to mourn the dead.

"This is an odd occasion. Should I be wearing a dress fit for a funeral? I didn't bring anything suitably somber." Vera assessed her wardrobe while Anna admired the black silk kimono Vera had been wearing the night before.

"And whose fault is that?" Rosemary said, somewhat sharply. "You took everything that would have been acceptable out of my case before we left. Would it have killed you to leave well enough alone?" She felt terrible as soon as the words left her lips, and even worse when Vera's face fell.

"I'm sorry," Rosemary said, sighing and touching her friend's hand lightly. "I'm a bit distraught, and honestly, I don't think Cecily would care what we wore, so long as we're there to bid her goodbye."

The response satisfied Vera, who patted Rosemary's arm. "It's all right, Rosie. I know how hard this must be on you, feeling as if you are obliged to accompany Cecily home, and yet needing to stay and solve the mystery." She didn't have to mention that ever since Andrew had passed, every death of someone close to her affected Rosemary deeply, and that alone was enough to bring on a dreary mood.

Still, Vera thought, it had been two days now, and she'd have to find a way to shift Rosemary out of the doldrums before the sadness became a habit. She noticed Anna fingering the kimono and said gently, "you can borrow that if you like, though I'm not sure it's appropriate for today."

"Thank you, Miss Vera, it's lovely," Anna said, though the thought didn't seem to cheer her.

"What's the matter, dear?" Rosemary asked. "Are you nervous about today? You won't have to see the body, you know."

"Really?" she brightened.

"Really. It's not a funeral, we're just accompanying her coffin to the ship. You don't have to go if you'd prefer not to."

Anna considered. "I didn't know Miss DeVant all that well, and to be honest, I've been dreading the thought. Are you sure you won't mind?"

"Of course not," Rosemary said.

Anna thanked her and tottered off to her own room holding the prized kimono.

"You're being quite lenient with her," Vera commented, but Rosemary had already slipped into the loo to finish dressing. Under her breath, Vera muttered, "I do hope she's being careful."

A half-hour later, in the most somber outfits they could find, the two women descended to the reception area where Frederick and Desmond waited in silence. Rosemary gratefully took her brother's outstretched arm and allowed him to lead her to the bus parked outside.

As more and more people lined the road to say goodbye, it became clear that during her short time in Cyprus, Cecily DeVant had touched a great many lives. Not only did all off-duty staff appear, but so did some of the guests, along with a host of people from the village who wished to pay their respects.

The ride back to the ship was somber, which would have infuriated the woman it was intended to honor. When Cecily's coffin was carried below decks, Rose breathed a sigh of relief.

The worst part was over; now came the memorial, which was to be held back at the hotel.

"Mrs. Lillywhite!" Gloria flagged Rosemary down as soon as she walked back into the lobby. "I have a telegram for you." She handed over an envelope, which Rosemary pocketed after giving Frederick a pointed look.

"It's from Mother and Father," she said, to which he nodded. The foursome found a quiet corner and Rosemary ripped open the envelope and read the contents aloud.

"Devastated. Stop. Stay. Stop. Investigate. Stop. Love Mother. Stop."

A woman of few words, Evelyn got her point across.

Frederick raised an eyebrow. "It seems they're coming around, doesn't it?" he asked. "Who would have thought Mother of all people would want you involved in a murder investigation?"

"I'm not surprised at all," Vera replied. "I believe your mother is far more progressive than she'd like to admit."

Coming from Vera, who had never got along well with Evelyn Woolridge, it was a high compliment.

Rosemary snorted. "I think you're the first person to ever call our mother progressive, that's for certain. At least we know they're supporting us, though I imagine it's more that mother is grieving and angry."

"Mother did always speak so highly of Cecily. I'm sure it was a blow to hear she's gone," Frederick agreed. "Now, let's just get through this afternoon. I fear it's going to be a long one." He wiggled his eyebrows at Desmond and caused Rosemary's hackles to rise.

"What are the two of you planning?" she asked, not sure if she really wanted to know the answer.

"None of your business, sister dear," was all he would say on the subject. Desmond merely shrugged, but a smile played around his lips. "Now, if you'll excuse us, we have some sleuthing to do."

With that, he and Desmond took themselves off to chase down their own theory of the crime. Smiling wryly, Rosemary watched them go. With their heads together as they conspired, Desmond's dark against Freddie's fair color, they reminded her of the young boys she remembered so full of mischief.

Rosemary and Vera settled into a table at the far corner of the lounge, one that boasted a vantage point that allowed them to observe the entire room and also make a hasty escape should one become necessary. Getting caught up in idle conversation with, say, one of the old biddies was not something either of the women wanted to endure. If Vera had to hear another word about rheumatism, her head would explode.

She peered at Richard Wright, who sat alone, his eyes on the door, watching like a hawk in much the same manner as Rosemary.

"You do realize, don't you, that Cecily's killer is among us at this very moment." The quiver of anger in Rose's voice sent a shiver over Vera's skin. "And I haven't a clue who it is."

"If you ask me, it's that Geneviève woman," Vera said, glaring at the subject of her ire from across the room. It was an abrupt change from her previous conviction that Richard Wright was the culprit, and Rosemary had a feeling she knew exactly why the French fiancée was on Vera's mind.

"Why? Because she'd have liked to take Freddie for a spin if he'd been willing?" Rosemary's eyes traveled to where Geneviève sat alone, *her* eyes trained on something else entirely: Benjamin leaning down to speak to Charlotte, who sat at another table. He smiled that smile of his that made Rosemary sick to her stomach, wiggling his eyebrows suggestively.

"Nothing of the sort," Vera said indignantly, bringing Rose back to their conversation with a start. "Freddie is free to demean himself however he pleases. Why should I care if his tastes run to rhinestones instead of diamonds?"

Why indeed, Rosemary thought, but she let Vera think she was fooled. "I'm sorry this hasn't been the holiday you expected. Days under the sun, nights of jazz and dancing. So much for romance on the Isle of Love."

Vera heaved a sigh. "I can have romance every night of the bloody week if I want it. Have done, really." Another sigh. "I think I'm getting old, Rosie. I'm losing my taste for the scandalous life. Living for the flutter and flash is losing its appeal."

Sagely, Rosemary only nodded, for until Vera figured the truth out for herself, she'd bite the head off anyone who ventured to point out she might be ready to think about settling down.

"It's these men today, Rosie, make no mistake. They're merely boys playing at the game of—"

A commotion interrupted Vera mid-sentence. An angry male voice rose and drew everyone's attention. Rose turned just in time to see Benjamin, back at his own table, slamming his fist down hard enough to make the cutlery jump. Geneviève started, and Rose watched in fascination as she smoothed the hint of fear from her face and replaced her expression with one of bored disinterest.

"I wonder what that was all about." Vera slid her tumbler back and forth on the table.

Rose shrugged. "I only caught a word or two. Probably just a little touch of jealousy on Geneviève's part, but I must admit I find it easier now to imagine him picking up a weapon and bashing Cecily over the head."

"Speaking of," Freddie said, appearing as if from nowhere and pulling out a chair. "Boothe says the murder weapon was probably a brass doorstop. You've seen them, they're shaped like a pineapple, and there's one in every room, so he's got men going door to door looking for one with bloodstains on it. He's certain he's going to catch his killer within the hour."

Tipping her glass, Rosemary sipped and hoped Freddie was right. She didn't care who caught Cecily's killer as long as justice was served. Inspector Boothe stood alone near the lounge entrance, watching the gathering with flat, expressionless eyes.

From time to time, one of his men would return with information, and from what Rosemary could tell, things weren't going to plan. With each short conversation, Boothe's brows furrowed a bit more.

"Where's Des?" Vera noticed the absence first. It had been the three of them more often than four, so Rose hadn't even thought of him. Whether that boded ill for their burgeoning relationship, or if she was simply distracted with grief, Rosemary

91

wasn't sure. What she did know was that she would not be rushed, and if Desmond couldn't understand her position, that was answer enough.

"Stopped to talk to one of the constables," Frederick explained. "Should be along once he's finished pumping the fellow for inside information about the case."

"No, no, no!" Another angry outburst near the kitchen door drew everyone's attention to Benny. "This is all wrong. It's all wrong."

As best anyone could tell since Benny capered in front of the buffet fairly blocking the view, someone had laid out the service differently than was Cecily's preferred arrangement, and Benny wasn't having it. His voice rose higher until Walter appeared and told him to hush up.

With a great deal of patience, Walter listened to Benny, whose face was flushed and sweaty in his earnest attempt to set things to rights. Rosemary found herself surprised by the patient way Walter calmed and diffused the situation.

Instead of chastising the younger man, he called one of the waitstaff over for a short conversation that resulted in the service being reset. Calmer now, Benny subsided and went off to do whatever it was that he did when there was no luggage to carry about.

Focused on Benny, Rose hadn't noticed that Desmond had finally joined the group. When she turned back and his eye caught hers, she blushed and looked away. Eventually, she would have to smooth things over with Des, but now was not the time. Besides, Des had news.

"There's been a theft of money. Boothe thinks he's found the motive for Cecily's death."

"Do tell, old chap," Frederick urged. "Sounds like we're one up on the girls, eh?"

"I had it from one of the constables that the little maid told him a sum of money had gone missing from Cecily's desk drawer a week, maybe two weeks back. She called all the staff in, lined them up, and gave a speech."

In triumph, Des snatched up Vera's drink and drained it off before telling the rest of his story. "The upshot of it all was that

92

she would let the matter lie for one week, and at the end of that time, if the money found its way back into the drawer, that would be the end of it."

"And was it? The end, I mean. Did the money come back?" Vera wanted to know, but Des clammed up as Walter approached the table.

"I just wanted to apologize on Benny's behalf. The boy is quite upset. He didn't mean anything."

Amid a chorus of reassurance that they'd suffered no ill will from the outburst, Walter asked after Anna. When Rose merely shrugged, he left to continue on his way towards the reception desk where he seemed to spend much of his time, flirting.

By then, Boothe had gone, and one of the guests started a trend by standing up to speak a few words about the dearly departed. For the next hour, guests and staff alike shared memories and stories that Rose would take back to her mother to help assuage the grief, for they portrayed Cecily as a woman of many facets. One who was kind yet firm, strict yet willing to help anyone in need.

Tears flowed as freely as the booze at the bar, and the mood at the end was one of both joy and sadness, but then, Rosemary thought, life is like that on the best of days.

Chapter Fourteen

When Rosemary and Vera approached the outdoor bar later that evening, they found it packed to the gills. It seemed everyone needed a reprieve from the sadness of the day. Taking a page from Vivi Chevalier's book, Gloria preened in front of the men, leaning in to talk to Desmond as though they were the best of friends.

"That woman has positively no scruples," Vera spat as they approached, echoing Anna's earlier statement regarding Benjamin Marlowe. "Not that anyone around here seems to have any. She's despicable, that's what she is."

"Oh, Vera, calm down. First of all, don't act as though you've never been forward with a man before because I've witnessed many a scene just like this involving some besotted fellow who was another woman's beau. Second of all," Rosemary continued, holding up her index finger to shush her friend, "if Desmond is stupid enough to fall for her charms, I don't want him anyway. Thirdly, I don't know if I want him at all."

Vera shot her a cold look. "It's not my fault if a man isn't happy with his woman. I've simply given a few of them a better option, but I've never turned my eye on a man who was engaged, and you know it. Moreover, Rosie, dear, it doesn't matter if you

94

want Des or not. We need to keep our little group close, especially considering how often we land in mortal peril!"

"You're being quite dramatic, *Vera dear*. Are you finding yourself missing the heat of the stage lights already?" Rosemary quipped, but her smile belied any malice behind her words. For the moment, she'd pushed Cecily's grisly murder from her mind and was attempting to put herself in a better mood. Needling Vera out of a fit of pique fit the bill.

"Perhaps. I've been thinking about my next role, and I've decided a bit of drama is in order. Modern drama this time, not of the Shakespearean milieu. But we can talk about that on the train ride home. For now, let's see how much damage we can do."

This time, her gaze landed on Frederick who, in a rare moment, didn't have a woman clinging to his arm. Rose shook her head and kept her mouth closed. Pushing Vera in any way would result in the opposite outcome she intended, which was somewhat ironic considering how pushy her friend could be when she thought she knew what was best for someone else.

"Let's do keep our heads about us, shall we?" Rosemary suggested. "Remember how ridiculous Geneviève and Benjamin looked when they had that blow up the other night. I'd rather hold on to a shred of my dignity."

"Speaking of the devils," Vera replied, "there they both are, wrapped around one another as though nothing happened."

Sure enough, the couple in question held court at the bar, Geneviève evidently telling a hilarious story that had her gesticulating wildly while Benjamin grinned from ear to ear.

Rosemary and Vera approached, Vera's eyes shooting daggers at Gloria, who returned the glare when Desmond turned his back on her to greet them. Neither said a word but held the stare until Gloria finally flushed and turned away. Satisfied, Vera tucked into her drink and tilted her head back to stare up at Freddie.

"What have we here? The great Lothario alone at the bar. Did you go through all of the available women already?"

As always, Freddie gave back as good as he got.

95

"I haven't noticed the male population prostrating themselves at your feet lately. What's the matter? Lose your touch?"

Before she could utter a scathing retort, a woman's voice interrupted her.

"Bonjour, mes amies," Geneviève had approached and made a big show of planting air kisses on Rose, Des, and Vera's cheeks, but her lips met Frederick's face and lingered there a touch longer than necessary. It was enough to turn Vera's sour mood bitter, and the fact that it irked her made her angrier still.

While Vera fumed, Rosemary greeted Geneviève and attempted to pull her attention away from Freddie. "It seems as though you and your fiancé are in a better mood tonight," she said, the words popping out of her mouth before she had a chance to censor them as she normally would. Rose found she cared little and rather enjoyed the look of irritation that crossed Vivi's face before she laughed and brushed the comment aside.

"Ah, yes, well, who amongst us hasn't been drawn into a lover's quarrel or two?" Geneviève replied.

"Where is Benjamin?" Rosemary asked, looking around and discovering he'd disappeared. A vague thought that too much gin had loosened her lips flitted across her mind. "Off hunting for more maids to torture, is he? Or perhaps another woman to proposition."

That was enough to make Vera hiccup beside her, Frederick's face turn beet red, and Geneviève's eyes to flash. "You silly English women think you're so evolved, but you obviously don't know a thing about relationships. Men are wild creatures who need to retain a semblance of freedom. Some women are the same way." She batted her eyelashes at Frederick, and the tension ratcheted up another notch.

"We *silly English women* actually have class," Vera retorted.

Geneviève smiled smugly now, her dig having struck gold. "Men don't appreciate class as much as they'd like you to believe they do. They appreciate guts and guile far more. Isn't that right, Frederick?"

The poor man looked like a gazelle who'd noticed the lioness just a moment too late. "Well, we appreciate a great many

96

things about you ladies." Freddie stammered, and turned wide, pleading eyes on Rosemary.

"Ah, perhaps I was wrong about you." Geneviève's hand, which had been poised to brush a lock of Frederick's curly blond hair back into place, went limp and dropped to her side. "I suppose you and your actress deserve one another."

Vera growled. It was a sound Rosemary had heard before, and one that meant she'd hit her limit. Vivi, having no idea what was coming, let a feral smile slip into place right as Vera hauled back a hand and slapped it off her face. Eyes widening with shock above the reddening handprint, Geneviève only missed a single beat before returning the favor, and then it was on.

Vera's fingers latched like vices in the French woman's hair, yanking and pulling the perfectly coiffed waves to tangled strands.

A collective intake of breath ran through the crowd, but no one stepped in to stop the fight, which ended fairly quickly anyhow when all the bravado deserted Geneviève, and she begged Vera to stop. Panting, sweaty, and close to tears, Vivi stumbled away while Vera crossed her arms and watched. Both women's eyes shone with moisture, but in Vera's case, the tears were the result of the sniffles, and not of ire or pain.

From where Rosemary was sitting, the Isle of Love truly did seem more like the Isle of Lust. Or perhaps the Isle of Crazy People, she wasn't sure which.

She linked arms with Vera and steered her towards the path leading back to the hotel. "I'm sorry about that. I should have kept my thoughts to myself. Perhaps I've gone round the bend," she mused. "So much for keeping our dignity."

Vera laughed. "Rosie dear, this was the most fun I've had all week. That woman deserves whatever she gets. She's a shameless, two-bit gold digger and someday it's going to come back around to bite her in the rear."

"I, for one, applaud you both," Desmond said jovially. "That was fine entertainment, don't you think, Freddie?"

Frederick smiled, but it didn't quite reach his eyes. He appeared to have a lot on his mind.

"Well," a voice said out of the darkness, making Rosemary's arm hair stand on end. She felt a little thrill vibrate through her body. "I have to say I agree with Desmond on that point. You ladies put on quite a show."

Chapter Fifteen

"Max!" Vera shouted while Rosemary gaped at the man standing in front of her. His presence on Cyprus was so unexpected she was struck dumb. Her heart thumped in her chest, and all the feelings she'd been pushing down came back to bubble up into her throat. "What are you doing here?" Vera demanded.

"I heard you'd landed yourselves some more trouble." It sounded like a reprimand without any real heat behind it. His eyes remained locked on Rosemary's. "I didn't realize it had come to fisticuffs. Arguing over a man, it sounded like."

His gaze flicked between Rosemary and Desmond, a neutral expression hiding the angst beneath. He'd worried her affections would be won during the trip out of London, and now it looked as if his worst fear might have come true.

To Rosemary, it appeared as though he couldn't care less, and her heart sank unexpectedly. Vera probably would have seen behind Max's mask if she hadn't been busy watching Frederick's reaction to his comment. Freddie, in turn, avoided her gaze along with his feelings. All five of them were drowning in subtext, including Desmond, who was the only one not thrilled about Detective Inspector Maximilian Whittington's arrival in Cyprus.

Finally, Vera came to her senses and answered Max's open-ended question. "That woman has been fawning all over every man who crosses her path, and she's engaged to a man even more promiscuous than she is. It's despicable. I simply put her in her place."

It hadn't looked simple to Max, and he also noted that the woman to whom Vera referred had managed to get in a few jabs of her own. "Rose," he said, looking at her expectantly, as she'd yet to utter a word.

"I'm just so shocked to see you here," she said, finally recovering her sensibilities. "It's wonderful, really." She gave him a somewhat awkward kiss on the cheek and then resorted to small talk. "What room are you staying in?"

"A few down from Frederick and Desmond, according to the receptionist," Max replied. "Would you like to get a drink and have a chat before we all retire for the evening?"

Rosemary agreed, ignored the brow wiggle Vera aimed in her direction, and followed him into the lounge after bidding goodnight to her brother and a sullen Desmond.

Once Rose and Max settled into a dimly lit corner table, the tension began to drain away, allowing the pair to return to their normal rhythm.

"Are you all right?" Max asked now that they were alone.

With a nod and a sigh, Rose replied, "I'm fine, but trouble and tragedy seem to follow me everywhere lately. This time, it happened to someone I actually knew and cared about. Cecily was a wonderful woman and a great friend to my mother. It's more than a pity. It's an injustice I intend to rectify." Her jaw set determinedly, turning her face into a fierce mask that Max couldn't help but admire.

"I'm sorry for your loss, Rose. I got on the train as soon as I received word from the local police."

"And your mother? Is she angry that you left just as she was moving into her flat?" She'd met Max's mother once before and come away with the distinct impression the woman didn't care for her. She could only imagine what Mrs. Whittington would think about her son running off to Cyprus to her aid.

Max kept his face neutral. "Mother is just fine, especially considering she's currently on a trip with a group of her lady friends. She didn't spend more than two nights in her new home before running off to Bath. It seems she has embraced her retirement and is taking to the waters for her health. That is a direct quote."

"I suppose she knows what's best," Rosemary smiled.

"What is your take on this murder? Do you have a suspect?" Max asked.

Rose scrunched her nose and said, "Several. That's the problem. Very few of her employees cared for Cecily, and they all seem to have cause to want her out of the picture. I've got a line on a couple of the guests; a man named Richard Wright, who has been pushing for her to persuade the owners of the hotel to sell. I certainly wouldn't put it past him to resort to violence, but all I've seen him do so far is make petty complaints and issue empty threats."

Max nodded as if he knew the type.

"Then there's the woman Vera just put in her place. She also seems to have detested Cecily, though for what reason I'm not sure. Geneviève Chevalier is engaged to a man named Benjamin Marlowe, and he's a shady character if I ever met one. What either of their motives might be, I haven't a clue. There's very little hard evidence pointing in any definitive direction, save for the threatening letters we found in Cecily's handbag." Rose explained what the letters contained while Max listened. "They were typed with no signature, and I've been unable to track down the machine on which they were made. Basically, I'm at a dead end."

"You look exhausted." Max rubbed at his chin, and Rose heard the scrape of whiskers against his fingers. She looked at him more closely and saw the fatigue that hovered over his own features even as he worried about her.

"Dear Max, that is surely a case of the pot calling out the kettle on account of its color. You look like you haven't slept for days."

"The fastest way from London is to travel with freight, or as freight, I suppose. Not much luxury to be had, but plenty of speed. I'm not sure if I've caught up with myself yet."

But he'd come for her, and Rose found herself incredibly touched by the gesture. Enough that she nearly kissed him but caught herself in time to avoid being made the fool.

"Why don't we reconvene in the morning and figure out where to go from there." If Max was aware of her impulse, he never let on. "I'd hoped you'd find some peace on this holiday, Rose."

"I have, Max, found some in the midst of all this. Now that you're here, well, I have to say I'm feeling much better."

She didn't tell him her heart had been going pitter-pat ever since he'd arrived. She didn't say any of the things she wanted to say and neither did he, but he walked with her towards the lobby, a protective hand on her back.

Rosemary was surprised to see Gloria standing behind the reception desk, looking even more sour than usual. "Are you all settled in, Mr. Whittington?" she asked, batting her eyelashes at him while staunchly avoiding Rosemary's gaze.

"Yes, thank you," Max said, not taking his own eyes off Rosemary.

"You don't usually work evenings," Rose commented, unwilling to allow the impertinent girl to disregard her., She was surprised to see Gloria back behind the desk after having spent most of the evening guzzling cocktails and flirting shamelessly.

Gloria raised her eyes up towards the ceiling. "I do since I had to give Margaret a night off and dock her pay. It is my job to fill in when I am needed."

"Really? She seemed like a good girl." Rosemary's stomach churned, hoping she and Vera weren't the cause of someone losing their job.

"Yes, well, good employees don't allow keys to go missing from the office during their shift."

Rosemary's heart sank, her suspicion confirmed. As disgusted as she was that Gloria would speak that way in front of guests, she wasn't shocked. If Cecily's uncle didn't find another decent manager to run the hotel, she had a feeling Richard Wright might be correct in his estimation that the Aphrodite was in trouble.

"You'll have to take the stairs," Gloria said as they turned to leave. "The lift isn't available at the moment."

Rosemary dreaded the thought of walking up three flights but quickly resigned herself to the task. To her surprise, someone was rummaging around in the supply closet where Cecily had died, and when Richard Wright's head popped out from behind the door, she wondered if her thoughts had summoned the man.

"Oh, hello there," he said, somewhat guiltily. "I'm just looking for some fresh towels since the maid doesn't seem intent on bringing me any. The door was open," he explained even though neither of them had asked.

"All right," Rosemary replied. "Have a good night."

"I'm sure I will now that I've taken matters into my own hands," Wright said.

Arriving back at the suite, Rosemary found Vera exactly where she expected her friend would be: sprawled across the sofa with a drink in her hand waiting to hear what had transpired with Max.

"Spill," Vera ordered and raised the tumbler to her lips.

It wasn't spite, exactly, that made Rose hesitate, more the need for a moment to ponder. "Where's Anna?" she stalled.

"She's out with the friends she's made since we got here. I told you that situation was going to get worse before it got better," Vera said, echoing her previous statement regarding Anna. "You need to watch that girl, or she'll get herself into trouble."

Not the level-headed, somewhat timid girl, Rose knew. Anna wasn't possessed of an intrepid soul, but of the type of personality to sit on the sidelines and watch others commit daring deeds.

"That reminds me," Rosemary said. "I think Anna has set her sights on that assistant manager chap, Walter." She explained how she'd seen Anna looking at him the morning after Cecily's murder.

"She aims too high. A man of his station would never go for a common maid," Vera said. Her eyes widened when she realized how insulting her comment was, and she shook her head emphatically. "Not, mind you that he could do any better than our

Anna. I only meant, from his perspective, she wouldn't be a fitting choice for anything but a minor dalliance."

The possibility of which Vera had warned Rose since they'd arrived.

"Walter is the type of man who worries more about how his actions are perceived than how they are intended. He'd consider his status and whatnot to be of more import than Anna's tender heart. He'd sooner go for one of those diamond-encrusted heiresses that would never look twice at him."

Wincing, Vera drained her glass and ignored the pang of remorse when she realized she *was* one of those diamond-encrusted heiresses, regardless of whether or not she'd ever acted like one.

Rosemary's heart thudded in her chest as a new thought occurred to her. "You're right, Vera. I hadn't considered until just now—"

"That I might be right about something?" Vera asked sharply. "Thank you for the vote of confidence."

"What? Oh, no, Vera, that's not what I meant. The interaction between Charlotte and Benjamin Marlowe has been bothering me. It seemed strange that a man whose fiancée looks like Geneviève does would want to flirt with a girl like Charlotte."

Rising, Rose went to the bar cart and poured gin into the bottom of a tumbler. Taking a sip for fortitude, she added, "You must admit, she's rather too plain for Benjamin's seeming tastes, though saying so right out makes me feel uncharitable. However, it's just as you said—he would never go for a common maid."

"It does seem strange, though what his behavior towards Charlotte implies I couldn't guess," Vera replied.

Rose rested her chin in her hand and stared off into the distance. "It implies they have some sort of connection of which we're unaware. Or, she was telling the truth when she said he was simply lodging a complaint." She shook her head emphatically. "No, that can't be right. Charlotte was lying about something, of that I'm positive. I thought it might have to do with Cecily's murder, but perhaps not."

"It's a line to tug." Vera dismissed the subject and moved on to the one that had her most curious. "For now, I want to tug on the Max line. What happened between the two of you? He couldn't take his eyes off you, you know." Vera's words brought a blush to Rosemary's cheeks.

She brushed aside Vera's comment. "We talked mostly about the investigation. I filled him in on what's happened so far, but he was tired from traveling, and we decided to discuss it again in the morning. Did you know he came here on a freighter or possibly a series of them?"

Vera took in that piece of news without so much as a flicker of surprise. "If he thought you were in danger, I've no doubt the man would sprout wings and fly."

"Don't be silly." Rose fluttered a hand at Vera and rose to put her tumbler back on the cart.

"Don't be naive," Vera countered, and then gave in. "It has been one more long day in the midst of many. Let's get some sleep, shall we, and maybe we'll be more clear-headed in the morning."

CHAPTER SIXTEEN

"Rose! Rosemary!" The urgency in Vera's voice roused Rosemary from her dreams, and she woke with a start.

"What?" she snapped, glaring at Vera. She'd finally slept without being plagued by nightmares, though the rude awakening had obliterated whatever lovely dream it was she'd been having. Rather than deal with the implications of her nightmares dissipating on Max's arrival, she tried to focus on what Vera was saying.

"I heard a noise, some sort of disturbance. Get up. Let's go find out what's happening." Her eyes were brighter than they ought to have been, considering the early hour. It couldn't have been later than five o'clock in the morning, and neither of them had fallen asleep more than a few hours before.

Rosemary propped herself up on her elbows and yawned. "I'm sure it's nothing," she said.

"It's not nothing! Can't you hear the commotion?"

"No, and I never shall if you won't stop talking."

"Something is wrong. Now, get up, or I shall have to go and investigate alone." Vera was not above using logic or coercion to get what she wanted.

"Leave off," Rose exclaimed when Vera yanked at the bedclothes. "I'm getting up."

The pair dressed hastily and sneaked out of the room, taking care not to disturb the soft sounds of Anna's snores. She must have come in late, though if the sounds emanating from the hallway failed to stir her, Rosemary thought nothing would.

Guests lined the hallway, all peeking out of their rooms to see what the fuss was all about. Someone had opened the stairwell door, and bodies clogged the entrance. The wail of a distraught woman echoed from below, and Rosemary's ears pricked.

She looked sideways at Vera. "That sounds like Gloria."

Someone tapped on Rosemary's shoulder and she turned with a start. Max was standing there, Frederick and Desmond behind him.

"Clear the way," Max said, taking charge of the situation. His tone, one of supreme authority, brooked no refusal, and the crowd parted to allow the five of them to descend the staircase. At the bottom, they found Gloria huddled beneath a blanket that had been pulled haphazardly from the supply closet, leaving a pile of linens strewn on the floor. Walter knelt beside her while Richard Wright hung back watching the scene play out with an enigmatic expression on his face.

"What happened?" Max asked gently, bending down to examine the woman.

Gloria began to cry with great, wracking sobs that shook her entire body.

"Someone attacked me!" she finally wailed. "I was in here looking for fresh shaving soap for Mr. Wright, and someone came up behind me and struck me on the back of the head." She touched her fingers to the spot, which brought a fresh stream of tears. "I must have been out for a few moments, and then Mr. Wright woke me up."

"I couldn't sleep, so I thought I would take the air," he explained somewhat defensively. "Gave me a start, I tell you, seeing her sprawled on the floor." As an afterthought, he added, "I never asked for shaving soap."

Max glanced at the door where they'd seen the man just a few hours prior, and then pointedly back at Rosemary. It didn't look good for him.

"Let's get you up." Max took one of Gloria's arms, Freddie the other, and gently lifted her from the floor. As they did, the blanket she'd been clutching fell, and Rosemary bent to retrieve it from the floor. As she did, she noticed an item lying there that made her suck in a breath. Surreptitiously, she palmed the brass lighter and slipped it into her pocket.

At Max's suggestion, Rose and Vera led a shaky Gloria to the lounge and settled her in a comfortable chair.

"Did you see who attacked you?" Max asked gently.

"It was probably *her*!" came a voice from the stairwell doorway. Rosemary whirled around to find Geneviève Chevalier and Benjamin Marlowe standing there. She had her finger pointed straight at Vera, and her eyes were spitting fire. "She came at me just last night," Geneviève continued. "Pulled my hair and struck me across the face. She's unstable."

Geneviève loosed a flurry of French, and Benjamin had to calm her down with a few whispered words. He didn't take his eyes off the sobbing Gloria, though.

"Are you insane?" Vera demanded, incredulous. "There's quite a difference between a catfight and sneaking up on someone from behind. If I wanted to attack Gloria, I would have done it in front of witnesses!"

Wishing Vera had thought before she spoke, Rosemary looked to Max in a panic.

"Everyone calm down," he said, but his words fell on deaf ears.

Geneviève straightened up to her full, considerable height, and glared down at Vera. "You probably killed Miss DeVant too!"

That sent Vera into more of a frenzy, and she struggled visibly with the effort of not giving Geneviève another swat with the flat of her hand. "You're the one pointing fingers, maybe it was *you*! You or your deplorable fiancé, come to think of it!"

"Enough!" Rosemary yelled, her voice higher and more piercing than Max's, which forced everyone to stop bickering. "Why on earth would Vera have killed Miss DeVant, or for that matter, why would she have attacked Gloria? She has no motive, and she's been asleep in our suite all night. We don't even know if Gloria was the intended victim. Didn't you say you were covering a shift for someone else?" She turned to Gloria, who nodded but didn't speak.

"Furthermore, the attack took place in the supply closet, which isn't a place the receptionist usually visits. It's possible someone lured Gloria in there, of course." She looked directly at Mr. Wright.

"Me?" he exclaimed. "What reason would I have for wanting to hurt this poor girl?"

Rosemary raised an eyebrow. "As for your motive, I couldn't say, but you had the opportunity. It was, after all, your call that prompted Gloria to go to the supply closet, and you keep odd hours. I've seen you from the balcony in my room, roaming about quite early in the mornings."

Mr. Wright glared hard at Rosemary. "I did not call down for shaving soap in the middle of the night. You're just trying to shift the blame from your friend onto anyone else. We only have your word she was in your room, and let me you ask this, was there another employee on shift at the time? That's where you ought to be focusing your suspicions."

"*Was* there anyone else on shift?" Rosemary looked at Gloria.

"No, not until half six when Charlotte and Benny were scheduled to arrive. Of course, it doesn't mean a thing. Most everyone who works here lives on the premises. We have staff quarters on the north side of the beach," she explained. "I just can't believe any of the people I work with would do something like this."

It was a naive statement, considering her boss had been murdered only a few days before, but Rosemary knew people tended towards denial when it came to such matters.

Before anything more could be said on the subject, the local police arrived, led by Inspector Boothe. He strode into the lounge and made a beeline for Gloria. "What seems to be the trouble here?"

"Inspector Boothe, it's a pleasure. I'm Detective Inspector Maximilian Whittington of the London CID." Max introduced himself, shaking the inspector's hand. "I contacted you regarding the death of Miss DeVant. It's good you've come, as these crimes are likely connected."

"Yes, yes, that's exactly why I *am* here. I would have sent a constable, but when I heard someone was assaulted at the Aphrodite, I thought it best to attend to the matter personally. Come along, now," Inspector Boothe said, pulling Max with him.

To say the way Boothe treated Max irked Rosemary was a gross understatement. Once the two men were out of earshot, she said to her friends, "Of course, Max is an asset. He's a man. I'm just a little woman, who couldn't possibly be of any assistance. Well, mark my words: he'll be sorry he underestimated me."

"Boothe really gets under your skin, doesn't he, Rose?" Desmond asked, his tone playful but his eyes serious.

"Of course, he does," Vera answered for her. "It's typical for a man to think a woman can't have looks *and* a brain. You two are no better, making silly wagers over who will find the killer," she spat, conveniently forgetting she'd been more than keen to take the bet.

Frederick clutched his heart. "You wound me! If we didn't find the two of you formidable adversaries, we wouldn't have bothered with betting in the first place."

Someone, probably Walter in his capacity as assistant manager, had sent for Margaret to cover the front desk. When the girl arrived, her eyes were wide as saucers. "Poor thing probably thinks she'll be next," Vera commented.

The guests who had been milling about the stairway had gone back to their rooms to discuss Gloria's attack, spreading the word so that by the time they began filtering down for breakfast, it was all anyone could talk about.

"It isn't safe here," someone murmured.

"Safe as anyplace else," another guest replied.

"I'd have to disagree with you there."

"Well I, for one, am checking out." This came from a middle-aged American man whose wife appeared to have spent some time sobbing over the dramatic events of the morning. Her eyes were red, and her face swollen and blotchy. "Come along, dear," he said, approaching the reception desk.

While Margaret puttered around doing the man's bidding, Richard Wright sauntered out from the office after, presumably, being questioned by the inspector and Max. "Mr. Robinson, are you leaving?" he asked.

"Right so, right so. Can't say it seems a safe place, what with murderers and the like roaming about. We'll find lodging at one of the other hotels on the island. Might not be as nice as this, but we won't worry about being killed in our sleep."

Richard Wright bade the couple safe travels, but when he turned around, Rosemary caught the smug smile that flitted across his lips. It seemed Mr. Wright's prediction of the hotel losing business was coming true, and his self-satisfied demeanor did nothing to convince Rosemary he wasn't the one who had attacked Gloria.

"Where is that Benny?" the receptionist asked, exasperated, as a dust-coated bus deposited a small group of new guests into the lobby. Some eyed the officers who stood flanking the stairwell door with concern.

"You'd all better get right back on that bus and go back to town," Mr. Robinson said loudly. "There's been a murder here already, and now, some poor girl was attacked this morning."

If she were as prone to violence as Vera, Rosemary would have liked to slap the satisfied smile off Mr. Wright's face.

CHAPTER SEVENTEEN

"Strange, isn't it, that Benny hasn't shown up for work this morning?" Frederick noted. "He's an odd one, but he seems to care about his job. Looks suspicious if you ask me."

"I thought you two were convinced Charlotte the maid is behind all this," Vera retorted with a derisive huff. "She was also supposed to be here, and I don't see her anywhere."

Desmond cleared his throat loudly. "Actually, she came in through the back door while you two were busy watching Mr. Wright egg on the surly man who checked out. Perhaps if your attention hadn't been focused on the wrong suspect, you would have seen her."

Rosemary stared at him with wide eyes. His tone was harsher than any he'd used with her previously, and she suspected the reason had something to do with Max's arrival in Cyprus.

"She appeared in quite some distress, actually," Frederick said smugly. "But we never said we thought she was in it alone. Benny is missing, is he not?"

"You're telling me you believe Charlotte and Benny are the masterminds behind Cecily's death and Gloria's assault?" Rosemary balked, but the lighter in her pocket might be proof that Frederick was right. "Charlotte can't find a towel in a closet full of them, and Benny is practically a child."

"A child in a very large man's body. She'd need some muscle to pull this off. Benny could be the perfect tool."

"Well, I don't believe it. We found no record of violence in Benny's file. He seemed to have genuine feelings for Cecily, and he has never even raised his voice in our presence. He's a gentle soul," Rosemary insisted.

"Where is he, then?" Desmond retorted.

Vera had watched the exchange between them, could feel the tension rising along with the temperature outside as the sun inched higher in the sky. "Why don't we just go find out?" She spat out the challenge without much thought.

Rosemary stood, crossed her arms, and stared Desmond down. "Why don't we, then?" he retorted.

She turned and marched out the front door of the hotel. Gloria had mentioned that the staff lodging was located on the north side of the beach, so she took a sharp turn and headed in that direction.

"Wait, Rosie. What's the plan?" Vera asked, speeding her steps to keep up with the pumping of Rosemary's long legs.

Rosemary flapped her arms in frustration. "We find him, we ask him," she said. "And then we lay this whole pile of nonsense to rest."

"Do you think coming right out and asking him if he killed someone is the best way to go about this?" Vera asked with more excitement than trepidation in her voice despite the question.

Rosemary sidestepped a large rock that had so far been spared the wrath of the sea, had yet to be ground into grit and become part of the beach itself.

"It's worked well enough for us in the past, hasn't it? I highly doubt Benny is going to murder us right there in his own quarters. I don't for one second believe he's capable of that kind of brutality. Besides, we have two bodyguards in case, for some reason, I'm wrong. When they'll learn to trust me, I'll never know." The last part was muttered under her breath, but Vera caught the gist of it.

"Rose, we have to be realistic," Vera said. "Benny was scheduled to work this morning; he was supposed to arrive right around the time Gloria was attacked, but he never showed up.

You can't deny it looks bad for him. He could have come in, bopped her on the head, and then ran."

"I don't see it," Rosemary replied. "I simply don't. I still think Richard Wright is our man. If only he would leave long enough for us to get into his room. He still has the most to gain."

She couldn't stop thinking about those threatening letters Cecily had received before she died. They weren't Benny's style of speech, nor did she think he had the means to own a typewriter.

What Vera felt was that Rosemary, as much as she might enjoy berating her brother, had one trait in common with him. Both were stubborn to a fault.

Frederick had spent all week focused on little Charlotte as his prime suspect and refused to see the evidence against anyone else. Rosemary was just as quick to defend Benny.

The difference was, now that Freddie had been presented with another option, he'd jumped ship faster than a rat with his tail on fire, while Rose wouldn't be swayed until she had absolute proof.

Fickle Freddie couldn't commit to a murder suspect any more than he could commit to one woman at a time. A flaw, to be sure, and one that Desmond seemed to share.

For now, the duo trailed behind the women while Frederick's gaze surveyed the area in a protective gesture. As they approached the area near the staff quarters, the landscape changed from pristine white sand to that of a darker shade. More large rocks and boulders dotted the expanse of seaweed-strewn beach. This was part of the property no guest was supposed to lay eyes on, but the view of the mountains rising out of the sea was just as spectacular as it was from Rose's balcony suite.

"Benny!" Rose called out as she approached the cluster of small cabins. Shrewdly, she cast an eye over each building and guessed which one was Benny's based on the neat and methodical placement of stacked rocks along the walkway. They reminded her of the way Benny piled luggage on his cart.

"Go hide somewhere you can hear us, just in case," Rosemary demanded of her brother and Des. "We'll have better luck getting him to talk if we're alone. Less intimidating."

114

With the thought that he was to be considered intimidating, Frederick agreed, pulling Desmond into a thicket of bushes near an open window.

Someone was moving around behind the cabin door, and when she rapped on it, the noise abruptly turned to silence. Another rap elicited a brief flurry of movement, and the third an abbreviated oath.

"Who is it?" came Benny's muffled, irritated voice.

"Benny, it's Rosemary Lillywhite and Vera Blackburn. From the third floor. Can we speak to you a moment?"

"Off duty. Ask Gloria to hunt down the other porter," he mumbled.

"We need to talk to *you*, Benny. It's rather urgent," Rose pressed. "Can we come inside?" She heard another thump and some shuffling before Benny finally opened the door.

"What do you want?" he asked unceremoniously but allowed them to step across the threshold. "Don't have any tea or I'd offer you some."

If Benny really *was* a murderous psychopath, he was certainly a polite one, though the way his eyes kept darting to the closed bedroom door made Rose somewhat uneasy.

"No, thank you," she and Vera replied in unison.

Rosemary perched on the edge of a well-worn sofa while Vera chose a fluffy looking chair. When she sat, her rear end sunk so far into the cushion it was unlikely she'd be able to get out without help.

"Why aren't you at work, Benny?" Starting off with simple questions seemed like the best plan.

"It's Stan's first day back after the accident. He works the mornings, and I work the afternoons. Didn't Miss DeVant—" He trailed off as he remembered Cecily was no longer in charge of the schedule. "Gloria knows."

"Gloria was attacked this morning, and something of yours was found nearby." She let the bald statement sink in, watched the realization dawn on Benny's face, and prepared for him to become angry. "Did you hurt Gloria? Or Miss DeVant?"

When he only frowned, she felt herself release a breath she hadn't realized she'd been holding in. This was not a murderer, and not for the first time Rosemary vowed to listen to her intuition rather than the mutterings of gossip.

"Gloria was attacked?" Benny looked genuinely confused.

"I found this," Rose said, holding out the bronze lighter, "on the floor near the supply closet after Gloria was attacked. Then, she said you were supposed to come in for the morning shift, and when you didn't arrive…well, it looks suspicious," Rosemary said.

Benny sat down and put his head in his hands. "She must have forgot Stan was supposed to work today. I always show up for my shifts." There was a long pause while his eyes clouded over. "I lost my lighter two days ago, and I'd never hurt Miss DeVant; she's the one who gave that to me," he finally said, swallowing heavily. "I wasn't even up at the hotel that night. I was here, in my cabin." His eyes flicked to the closed bedroom door again, and Rosemary's narrowed on him.

"Tell the truth, Benny," she said gently.

Vera reached over, gave Benny one of her million-watt smiles, and patted his arm, "Whatever your secret is, you can tell us."

Benny's shoulders slumped, and he sighed as though he'd been carrying the weight of the world on them. He walked to the bedroom door, opened it, and bent down. A tiny ball of fur catapulted from inside and into Benny's arms. The little dog licked his face, which turned up into a smile so heartbreakingly innocent that Rose felt her worries melt.

"I'm not supposed to have him here. It's against the rules."

Rose exchanged a look with Vera, a sudden and disturbing thought occurring to her. "Did Miss DeVant find out about him?" Her voice was filled with trepidation now, and though he lacked certain mental capacities, Benny's eyebrows quirked at her tone.

"Miss DeVant was also the one who found Alfie and gave him to me. You think I would have killed her over a dog?" It seemed to make him sad again, which in turn made Rosemary feel worse than if she'd kicked the puppy.

"Of course not, Benny," she said, apologetic now.

Benny picked up the puppy and sat down with the wriggling little bundle in his lap. Alfie turned around twice and laid down, looking up at his companion with love in his canine eyes. It wasn't hard to see why Cecily might have broken a hotel rule; she'd never seen Benny happier, and she guessed he didn't have much happiness in his life.

"She was walking one of the trails one day and found him. He was so small he could fit right in my hand. Must have been the runt and got left behind." It was something Benny seemed to identify with, though how such a hulking man could have started out life as a runt was difficult to imagine. "She brought him to me, and said as long as Alfie was quiet, I could keep him."

"That sounds like something Cecily would do," Rosemary agreed. She hadn't known the woman long, but she had no doubt she was correct.

Benny looked straight into Rosemary's eyes. "I was out walking Alfie when Miss DeVant was killed, but I wish I had been there. Maybe I could have helped her."

"You were not to blame for what happened," Vera said, continuing her role as the good cop in the scenario, but Benny didn't seem content.

"Can you tell us where you went and who you saw?" Rosemary asked, grasping at straws for some tidbit of information that might help them move forward and figure out who really did kill Cecily.

His eyes on the dog, Benny took a moment to think. "I went where I always go. To a little spot along the beach where the boulders make a circle." Rosemary knew exactly the spot he was referring to because it was the same one she and her friends had discovered their first afternoon at the hotel. The dog mess she'd noticed must have been Alfie's. "We like to go late at night because then Alfie can run around and make noise without bothering anyone. I saw Charlotte pop out of her cabin when I was on my way back, but she went back inside and didn't wave hello like she usually does." Benny's focus returned to Alfie, and it appeared the conversation was over.

"All right then. Thank you, Benny," Rosemary said and turned to leave.

117

"I hope you figure out who killed Miss DeVant. If I can help in any way…" were Benny's final words on the subject.

When Rosemary and Vera finally exited the cabin, Desmond and Frederick were waiting for them. They'd been listening through the window and already knew what had transpired, but that didn't stop Rosemary from bragging. "See, I told you it wasn't him."

"You don't know that for sure," Frederick sulked. "He could have been lying."

Rosemary rolled her eyes, "He's not, and furthermore, it puts a kink in your theory that Charlotte is the murderer. She was in her cabin, just like she said she was." With that, she turned her attention to what she considered a bigger issue. "What I can't understand is what sort of violence Gloria was referring to." Rose paused and thought back. "She said, '*that Ben fellow was in a right state last night.*' And then Walter said something along the lines of '*Could be he had another violent episode.*' I assumed the Ben fellow was Benny, but maybe I was wrong."

"She could have meant Benjamin Marlowe!" Vera exclaimed, finishing Rosemary's sentence.

"She certainly could have."

Ignoring the idea of Benjamin Marlowe completely, Frederick muttered something uncomplimentary under his breath, and pulled Desmond ahead, leaving the women trailing behind. "We have some finer points to discuss," he said as he sailed by, his nose stuck in the air. "See you later."

Chapter Eighteen

When Rosemary and Vera returned to the hotel, Benjamin Marlowe was nowhere to be found, and neither was Max. "He must still be in with the inspector," Rosemary commented.

Richard Wright, still appearing quite pleased with the fact that at least a few guests had checked out of the hotel, finished his breakfast and approached the reception desk. Rosemary checked her watch and realized the ordeal with Benny had taken less than an hour.

"Make sure you take down all my messages, girl," Mr. Wright said in his usual brusque manner. "I've got some business in town, and I'll be gone all afternoon."

"Leaving us the perfect opening to snoop around his room," Vera said under her breath. "Luck is on our side today." They made for the lift and asked the operator to return them to their floor. After he'd gone back inside and closed the door, they made a beeline for suite 305.

With no shame whatsoever, Vera did the honors of opening Mr. Wright's door using the stolen key from the front office. That poor Margaret had lost wages over the theft weighed heavily on Rosemary's conscience. The only reason Gloria hadn't let the woman go altogether was to save herself having to work round the clock. Once Cecily's murder was solved, Rose vowed to tell Gloria the truth, providing Gloria wasn't the culprit, of course.

119

The pair tiptoed inside and placed the 'do not disturb' sign on the outside of the door. "There, we ought not to be interrupted," Vera said with satisfaction. The suite was a duplicate of their room, complete with a coat cupboard near the entrance door. "I'll check the bedroom. You look around in here," Vera suggested.

Rosemary nodded in agreement and went to work searching the myriad cupboards and drawers large enough to hold a typewriter. The room appeared to be in perfect order, though it seemed more likely due to Mr. Wright's own efforts as opposed to Charlotte's, given the limits of her expertise. Not one cushion was out of place; no speck of dust dared mar the surface of any desk, table, or bureau.

When Vera opened the clothes cupboard, she found more of the same: perfectly ironed garments organized first by occasion and then by color, and three cases piled neatly next to a row of meticulously shined shoes. In the bathroom, soaps and shaving things lined up like soldiers next to a stack of uniformly folded towels.

"There's something wrong with this man." Vera's voice floated out to the other room, where Rosemary smirked at the observation.

"He's certainly particular, but we already knew that."

Vera lifted the covers to check under the bed and found the sheets tucked ruthlessly tight.

"What we need to find out is whether he's also a violent psychopath with homicidal tendencies," Rosemary mused.

"You sound like a psychology textbook, Rosie," Vera laughed. "Unfortunately, I don't see a typewriter."

"Neither do I," she replied absently. He traveled lightly, with only a few personal possessions dispersed throughout the room. On an end table lay a stack of old but gently worn books, each with its own bookmark. Rosemary stopped to examine two framed portraits that sat in a place of reverence on the desk. One, a family of three featuring a younger Mr. Wright and a woman holding a baby, was faded with time. The other, crisper and more recent, was of a little girl in a frilly dress with an angelic smile on her round face. Whoever else he might be, Richard Wright

120

someone this was a husband, a father, and perhaps even a grandfather, if Rosemary's assumptions were correct.

"There's nothing suspicious here at all," she finally had to admit. As soon as she spoke the words, she noticed a leather folio tucked beneath the desk. She hesitated, her fingers itching to take a peek inside, but her reluctance to further invade another's privacy warred with the compulsion. They'd only wanted to know whether Mr. Wright kept a typewriter, and since the folio wasn't big enough to hold one, their mission had ended.

A sound outside the door startled Rosemary out of her contemplation. "Vera," she hissed, "Someone's coming."

Vera poked her head out of the bedroom, and the pair exchanged looks of panic.

"Come here," Vera hissed and pulled Rosemary into the coat cupboard. They shut themselves inside in the nick of time and heard the snicking sound of the suite door closing.

"Maybe it's just the maid," Vera whispered hopefully.

"Shh," Rose replied, though she wished the same thing. If Charlotte had come to take care of Mr. Wright's room, she'd find little to do and would, perhaps, simply leave and allow them to escape this futile endeavor. She scooted slowly towards the back of the cupboard, her arms stretched out behind her for support. Something hard and sharp, most likely a nail, poked out of the pile carpet and took a swath of skin from Rosemary's hand. She stifled the urge to cry out and wrapped her skirt around her hand to keep the blood trickling from the scratch from staining the floor.

Barely daring to breathe, they waited, listening as whoever was in the room walked to and fro as if searching for something. When he cleared his throat, they knew it was Mr. Wright himself, and Rosemary's heart sank. There came a clicking noise, and the shrill ring of the phone followed by Mr. Wright's impatient tones. "What are you doing calling me here? Leaving messages with hotel staff?"

He paused, waited for an answer while Vera grabbed Rosemary's arm and squeezed. Though Rosemary assumed the gesture had something to do with the dire situation they had got themselves into, in actuality Vera felt a sneeze coming on and was trying desperately to remain quiet.

"No, I'm sorry, dear. I didn't mean to--" Mr. Wright paused. "Yes, I know the situation isn't ideal, but you have to be patient," he sighed.

"Yes, yes, I'm doing my best. What more do you want from me?" Apparently, *dear* had a long list because Mr. Wright was quiet for a few moments.

"How could I have predicted the family would request the body be sent back for burial and not send someone to attend the memorial?" Pause. "Yes, I know it has been weeks, but I thought I had a clear shot, and now I need to reassess. I assure you; I will find a way to close this deal so we can go home. Now, I was on my way to you when I got your message. Yes, yes, very good." Mr. Wright set the receiver back with less delicacy than a man as particular as he might normally have done and muttered under his breath.

He paced a few moments more and then opened the door to leave. Vera, unable to hold in the sneeze any longer, expelled one of her dainty squeaks and then clapped her hand over her mouth. Rosemary held her breath, but Mr. Wright stopped short and spun around to look for the source of the noise.

With trepidation because, after all, one person had been murdered and another one attacked within the week, he picked up a weapon and walked slowly back towards the cupboard. When he flung open the door brandishing a bright yellow brolly like a sword, his face screwed up into a scowl that was meant to appear formidable but was more akin to mortal fear, it was almost enough to make Rosemary laugh out loud.

"What on earth are you doing in my room?" he exclaimed once he realized he was in no immediate danger. "You two meddling women are trespassing. I'm calling the police!" He turned towards the telephone while Rosemary and Vera scrambled up from their spots on the floor.

"No, wait," Rosemary pleaded, attempting to reach out and stop him. When Mr. Wright turned around and caught sight of the blood on her dress, his face went as white as the sheets on his immaculately made bed.

He backed away from her, and asked, somewhat more gently, "Are you hurt? Is that why you were hiding in here?"

She could have lied, got away with the whole debacle, but instead took a more direct approach. "I'm hurt, yes, but it's just a scratch. We…well, we thought you might be the murderer. Or, at the very least, the person who had been trying to blackmail Cecily DeVant."

"Why that's preposterous," he retorted. His eyes rolled back when he caught sight of the blood for the second time.

This was not a man who was capable of murder, or at least not via the way Cecily had died. If he'd wanted her dead, he was far more likely to have slipped a bit of poison into one of her cocktails. Richard Wright simply didn't have the stomach for the kind of brutality that Cecily had endured.

"I didn't want the woman dead, and I certainly didn't blackmail her. I don't know what you're talking about. In fact, the whole idea is preposterous," he seemed completely taken aback as he repeated the assertion. "Believe you me, Miss DeVant had no skeletons in any of her cupboards. So far as I'm concerned, the only secret the woman had was who actually owns this hotel, and that information she took to her grave. The public records list a business name that, for all intents and purposes, is a front."

"Why are you so intent on buying a hotel that isn't for sale?" she demanded. Her hand had started to throb now that the adrenaline rush of being caught snooping had drained, and she was both irritable and past ready to return to her suite, clean herself up, and take a rest. "The letters we found in Cecily's handbag certainly sounded like they could have come from you."

He had the decency to look somewhat contrite, and Rosemary guessed he'd done enough research on her to know that for a fact. While he might not have actually resorted to blackmail in this case, he'd certainly considered it and only kept his conscience clean because he hadn't found anything incriminating enough to carry out his plan. Which begged the question of who, if not a conniving businessman, would have known where exactly to press Cecily.

Mr. Wright's forehead creased as he furrowed his brow, and suddenly he looked even older. "You young women these days think you can speak to your elders any way you like. Don't forget I could call the police and press charges against you, or at the very least have you removed from this hotel," he reprimanded. He might as well have shaken a finger at her.

"A course of action you would find more difficult than you think," Vera huffed, "now that we have a better idea of what you've been up to. I'd say we have more ammunition than you do, so why don't we just cooperate with one another?"

"You're certain the hotel is not available?"

"I am, and I have it on very good authority."

"Then, I am sunk. Cecily DeVant's death was a matter of great inconvenience to me."

"Have you any idea who killed her?" Rosemary asked bluntly, thoroughly irritated by the events of the afternoon and no longer remotely scared of Richard Wright.

The man sank down into the desk chair and heaved an enormous sigh as though defeated. "How on earth should I know?" he asked.

"You must have seen something or heard something that makes you think it's one person or another," Rosemary said, still awkwardly holding her bloody hand against her skirt. She shifted her weight to her other foot and vehemently wished he'd invite her to sit even though the circumstances of their presence in his room didn't dictate that he was required to do so.

"I was given to understand Miss DeVant had stepped in to run the hotel because the owner was in ill health and that it would likely go up for sale in the event of his passing. When I looked into public records, however, I was unable to find the owner's name."

Pausing, he waved a hand towards the nearby sofa. "Sit, please." Wright cleared his throat. "I thought if I could only speak to him, I could get him to sell sooner. Take the white elephant off his hands, as it were."

Rosemary cocked a brow at him. "While working steadily to drive the price down by undermining the hotel's reputation."

A dull red color crept up from beneath Wright's collar as Rose pinned his motive with deadly accuracy.

"Say what you like, but I've seen a great many things during my stay at this hotel. Discovering the two of you in my coat cupboard isn't even terribly shocking. Not, mind you, that I expect to find either of you poking around my room again."

His reprimand had weight behind it, but Mr. Wright was still taking their trespassing with surprising aplomb, especially considering his usual churlish demeanor. He crossed his legs and determined himself to brave out the accusation.

"As to the murder, it could have been any one of them. Yes, I suspect it could have been. Miss DeVant made it a point to harangue every single one of her staff at one point or another. Is it any wonder they all seemed to despise the woman?"

Having seen Cecily taking Gloria to task, Rose offered no argument.

"But would a public dressing down be a motive for murder?" Wright mused. "A rather extreme reaction, what? There are plenty of places to work on this island. Maybe none of the other hotels hold the same status as The Aphrodite, but..." he trailed off. "Though I suspect the young maid will struggle to live up to higher standards than she's been held to at this establishment."

"You can't possibly think Charlotte killed Miss DeVant," Vera said incredulously. It seemed everyone wanted to point the finger in her direction. "Especially if Cecily's death would put her in dire straits."

"I shouldn't think so, but as a seasoned traveler, I've stayed in hotels in every major European city, America, and the West Indies. Never have I seen the level of patience Miss DeVant showed that maid, with the exception of family ties. I don't believe little Charlotte is related to Miss DeVant, but I do believe there was some deeper connection between the two. Murder is often committed for personal reasons, don't you know?"

Having heard enough to know Mr. Wright hadn't a clue, nor was he responsible for Cecily's death, Rose stood to leave. "I'm sorry to have troubled you, and I'd like to thank you for being so patient with us after we invaded your privacy."

"Quite all right, young lady. No harm done." He graciously waved away the apology. "And you're quite certain the hotel will not be sold?"

"As certain as I can be." With that, Rose and Vera swept from the room with more information than they'd had going in, but also with more questions than answers.

Chapter Nineteen

Having learned his secrets, Rosemary and Vera exited Richard Wright's room to find Frederick and Desmond waiting outside the door of their suite. "What have you two been doing in there?" Frederick demanded before he noticed the blood on Rosemary's dress. "And what did he do to you?" If looks could kill, Richard Wright would have been dead right on the spot.

"Nothing, Freddie, calm down," Rosemary said, averting her eyes from Desmond's gaze. His face had turned bright red, and his fingers clenched at his sides. She still hadn't been alone with him and they'd hardly spoken since their kiss on the beach. Due, no doubt, to the poor way she'd handled the awkward moment, and probably to Max's arrival as well.

Seeing her hurt, however, softened his resolve even as he felt his blood rise up to a boil at the thought of anyone harming her. "I cut myself on a nail is all. I'm fine, I simply need a moment to get cleaned up."

Inside their suite, Anna's bedroom door was closed, and they could hear her moving around on the other side. By the time Rosemary had changed her clothes and allowed Vera to help her dress the wound on her hand, Max had arrived to round out the group.

He paced across the sitting room, his brow furrowed. "I've been looking for the lot of you for hours. Where have you been?"

127

"Well, first we were talking to Benny, the porter," Rosemary explained sheepishly. "He didn't attack Gloria or Cecily for that matter, but let's keep that to ourselves and let Inspector Boothe run around in circles."

"I don't know who Benny the porter is," Max reminded her. "I only arrived last night, remember?"

Rosemary accepted the gin and tonic Frederick pressed into her hand and grinned up at him. "Thank you," she said, for once thoroughly pleased that her brother always had a cocktail at the ready. "Benny is a big hulking man child whose deep, dark secret is that he's hiding a puppy in his staff cabin."

"Oh," Max said, catching up. "Gloria mentioned him, and she told the inspector that Benny was supposed to work this morning and never arrived."

"Yes, that's correct. The thing is, he says he had the day off and the other porter, the one who has been out of work due to an accident, was actually scheduled. An innocent mix up from the sounds of it, and of no concern to the case."

"We also managed to check Richard Wright off the list of suspects," Vera sounded quite pleased with herself. Rosemary sipped her drink and allowed Vera to tell the tale with all the pomp and circumstance of a trained actress.

"He could barely stomach the spots of blood on Rose's dress, let alone have bludgeoned Cecily to death. It would have taken someone with a strong constitution if not actual physical strength. Which also, one would assume, negates the possibility of it having been little Charlotte, the maid. She's a mere slip of a thing, after all."

She couldn't help but include the not-so-subtle dig in her retelling of the events of the afternoon, and though Desmond appeared to be having second thoughts about their number one suspect, her words didn't have the intended effect of extinguishing Frederick's conviction.

"You don't know that for certain, Vera," he said sharply. "Desperate people do desperate things. As evidenced by your brash attempt to break into Mr. Wright's suite."

Max cleared his throat loudly. "He's right, you know, and actually, Rose, these two may not be as far off base as you'd like to believe."

Vera snapped her mouth shut and stared at Max with barely concealed irritation. "What do you mean?"

"Well, Inspector Boothe came through with some information, and I've spent all afternoon communicating with London to confirm it. What it amounts to is this: Charlotte's last name is Marlowe."

Rosemary's sip of gin and tonic went down wrong, and after a bout of coughing, she exclaimed, "As in Benjamin Marlowe?"

"The same. She's his wife." He paused a moment to let the news sink in. "Apparently, she left him and then came down here to lay low. He's been looking for her for months. The missing person report ran across my desk, but I didn't make the connection until the inspector here in Cyprus filled me in." The fact didn't appear to please him, but he shrugged it off.

"I knew it!" Vera cried. "I knew she wasn't just a lowly maid." She flushed, grateful Anna was in the other room and hadn't heard the comment.

"Richard Wright said he thought there had to be a more personal connection between her and Cecily," Rosemary said thoughtfully. "Perhaps Cecily found out who she really was, and…but that doesn't make any sense. One would think, if that were the case, the blackmail would have worked the other way around."

"Unless," Desmond said, drawing out the word, "she's the one who was stealing money. Cecily tried to draw the thief out, promising that if the money was returned, she'd drop the issue. Let's say it was Charlotte; that would have given her reason to threaten Cecily. Those letters contained only threats, correct? No demands? Maybe Charlotte wanted Cecily to drop it so she could keep the money and run."

Anna's door creaked open behind the group, and a voice that wasn't hers spoke into the din. "Those are all very interesting theories, but unfortunately none of you have hit the nail on the head." Rosemary and her friends whipped around to see Charlotte standing with her hands on her hips, a snarl painted across her narrow face.

"Where did you come from?" Rosemary asked even as she figured out that it had been Charlotte in Anna's room the entire time, and that the girl had overheard everything they'd been saying about her.

"I'm a maid. I was doing my job. Cleaning up after the likes of you all day long wasn't exactly my life's ambition, you know!" Malice etched her face. Even though she'd denied the accusations against her, Charlotte looked, for the first time, as though she might have been able to carry out a grisly murder after all.

"If I'd stolen that money, don't you think I would have used it to get out of here? Why would I continue to do a job that I detest? And I didn't kill Miss DeVant, either. She was my friend," Charlotte said, her voice hitting a pitch so shrill Max put a finger to his ear and cringed.

"But that morning," Rosemary said slowly, "after I found the body when the police were about to question you. You said you didn't like Cecily." She thought back and realized that perhaps Charlotte hadn't quite said as much after all. "Didn't you?"

Charlotte snorted. "No, I didn't. *You* said nobody liked her. I didn't disagree, but that's because I was upset. Miss DeVant knew about my estrangement from Ben, and she felt sorry for me. She knew what it would mean—a *divorce"*—Charlotte spat out the word as if burned her tongue "to my family and to my friends. *Some* of us were raised with high morals and standards. Some of us don't subscribe to the theory that marriage ought to be tossed over just because a couple isn't as happy as they thought they would be!"

Frederick, apparently having come to terms with the fact that he might have been wrong—or perhaps scared that if somehow, Charlotte was still lying, she might make him her next victim—poured the girl a brandy. "Why don't you sit down and tell us what's going on," he said, attempting to lead her towards an armchair.

"No!" Charlotte cried. "I don't want a drink, and I don't want to calm down. All I wanted was to make my husband realize what a mistake he'd made. I thought, eventually, that he would tire of his debauchery, come find me, and bring me home."

A look of distaste mixed with pity crossed Vera's face. *What sort of modern woman would behave this way?* She wondered. It hadn't occurred to her that not all women were as modern as she was.

"Instead," Charlotte continued, "he brought that hussy Geneviève here with him, and tried to bribe me to petition for divorce." She was pacing at this point, and in such a tizzy that the hair pulled severely back from her face and wound into a bun had come loose. Tendrils of auburn spilled around her eyes, which were wild with rage. "All he wants is her money and to use her as a trophy. Believe me, if I were going to kill anyone, it would be the two-bit tramp who stole my husband!"

Rosemary wasn't sure quite what to say or how to handle the situation and was relieved when Max took control. "Charlotte, I'm sure we're all terribly sorry for what you've been through— and for good reason. If what you say is true, and you cared about Miss DeVant, perhaps you know something that might help us catch her killer."

"Well," Charlotte said, taking a deep breath and sinking, finally, into one of the armchairs. "That horrible Richard Wright was trying to put something over on Miss DeVant. I wouldn't put anything past him. He's spent the last two weeks terrorizing the rest of the staff and me. For what purpose I couldn't say, though I suspect it has something to do with money. As things so often do."

"Cecily had, in her possession, letters of a threatening nature. We know Richard Wright didn't blackmail Cecily," Rosemary explained. "He would have if he'd had the opportunity, but he couldn't find anything to hold over her head. Someone else must have had reason to write those letters though. They have to mean something."

"Do you still have them?" Charlotte asked.

Rosemary produced the clutch that held the stack of notes and handed it to Charlotte. "Cecily left this in our room the night before she was murdered. I suppose we should have handed them over to Boothe," she said when she saw the look on Max's face. "It just now occurs to me that we've withheld evidence."

Charlotte fingered the handbag, a puzzled expression on her face. "This isn't Miss DeVant's," she said. "It wasn't her style. I've seen it before, but I can't for the life of me remember where. Perhaps in one of the guest rooms..."

"If that's not Cecily's, then maybe the letters aren't hers either!" Rosemary exclaimed. "Could we have been chasing a dead end this whole time?" The new information forced her to look at things from another perspective. She began to pace the room, much as Charlotte had done, talking to herself as she did.

"We know it wasn't Benny; his alibi makes too much sense, and I just can't see him as the violent type. Richard Wright has too weak a stomach for murder. None of the other staff seem dissatisfied enough to resort to murder. I hate to broach the subject, but just how duplicitous is your husband?"

Charlotte hopped to her feet, the blood rising to her face. "It wasn't Ben," she snapped. "He was with me the night Miss DeVant was killed."

Max whipped his head around to face Charlotte, "All night?"

She shot him an indignant look, and spat, "He was still my husband, so if I had been with him all night, there would have been no shame to it. We were together until after midnight, and though I don't owe anyone an explanation, it wasn't a scandalous meeting." The blush rose to her cheeks again, and Rosemary tilted her head.

"Would he have liked it to be?" she asked, going with her hunch.

"He's a man," Charlotte responded without meeting Rosemary's gaze. "But he's not a murderer. His new *fiancée* proves his taste in women has declined, but there's no crime in chasing after the wrong skirts. Now, if you'll excuse me, I have a job to do." She gathered her cart from the other room and made for the door.

132

"If you remember where you saw that clutch, please let us know immediately," Rosemary implored the maid as Charlotte closed the door behind her.

Chapter Twenty

"As if my opinion of Benjamin Marlowe could have been any lower." Vera's lips twisted with disdain. "He's the lowest form of life."

"Huzzah!" Freddie said. "I've finally been bumped out of my prime position on your list of men to hate."

"Don't be too sure, Frederick Woolridge." Vera rounded on him. "There's plenty of room for you still. What makes you any different? You go through women like you go through good gin."

"The difference, Vera my love," Freddie said, smiling, but with no trace of his usual cheer, "is that I am footloose and fancy free, and therefore, am entitled to sample my share of the fairer sex. As you should well know, Miss Pot."

"Don't you paint me with your depraved brush, Mr. Kettle." The two squared off yet again. "I'm not the one cutting a swath through every available man on the island."

"Here, now. I haven't been out with *every* available woman."

Vera picked up on the implied insult, and her claws came out. "I'll amend my statement to only include the ones dimwitted enough to fall for your overblown charms. Why can't you be more like Des? Des is a gentleman. Look at how he handled the situation with Rosemary."

"What situation with Rosemary?" Max was the one who voiced the question, and Vera, her eyes still locked on Freddie's face, answered without thinking.

"When Des steals a kiss from a woman, and she's not sure how she feels, does he press the advance? No, he does what a gentleman does and gives her time to think about her feelings and lets her make up her mind in her own time."

Unaware of the rising tension in other parts of the room, Frederick stepped closer to Vera, so close his breath mingled with hers. "Trust me, Vera dear, if I decided to press my advance, you'd know how you felt about it without me having to give you time to think."

Vera shivered under the heat of Freddie's gaze, and after, couldn't say what might have happened next between them, but before anything could, the sound of Max's voice cut the moment short.

"You stole a kiss from Rosemary?"

The whole thing might have ended there, but Desmond's eyes fired up hot. "I did, and I plan to do it again if she'll have me."

Always quicksilver, Vera's mood went from incensed to intrigued, and she grinned up at Freddie. "I think I've put the fox among the hens."

If a fight broke out, Vera would put her money on Max as cold fury always trumped angry heat, but Rose wouldn't thank her for putting the match to the fuse on this powder keg. That fact was driven home by the daggered look Rose sent Vera's way.

"You put your foot in it good and proper now," Freddie whispered, but he made no move to step between the other two men. Nor did either of them follow the rules of polite society and withdraw for the sake of privacy.

"Stealing implies a lack of permission." Max fisted his hands at his sides and locked eyes with Rose. "Did he coerce you in any way?"

Rose shot another annoyed look in Vera's direction. "It was an innocent kiss, Max."

"By Jove, Rosemary," Desmond exclaimed, "when a man kisses a woman like you, he never means it to be innocent. You

135

make me sound like a yapping puppy jumping at your skirts, and what business does Max have in all of this? Are you tied up with him?"

Thoroughly on the spot now, Rosemary looked to Vera for guidance. Juggling men was her area of expertise, but Max answered the question first.

"Not in that way, but we are friends, and I take Rosemary's happiness quite seriously. What are your intentions towards her?"

Vera let out a sound that could have been taken for one of her precious little sneezes, but Rose recognized it as a snort. "Don't answer that question, Desmond." She turned to face Max. "Because it's impertinent. Who I kiss or don't kiss is nobody's business but my own."

Out of the corner of her eye, Vera noted the door to the suite opening and saw Charlotte peer around the edge and fix her gaze on Anna's door. She'd probably forgotten something when she'd been in earlier. Frowning, the maid seemed to be struggling with her dilemma, one Vera watched play out over her face. Biting her bottom lip, Charlotte sidled into the room, though what she did after, Vera couldn't say because she turned her attention back to see how Rosemary would handle the two men in her life.

"I'd like to know, too." Now Frederick jumped in. "Look, mate, you're my friend, but Rose is my sister. If all you want is a flutter, and she's game, then I'll stay out of the way. But don't think I won't have a go at you if you play around with her affections."

"That's it. Enough, Frederick!" Face flaming, Rosemary whirled on her brother. "All of this uproar over a single kiss. Get out. The lot of you. Just go away and let me have a moment to collect my thoughts. Go to the bar, get snockered, take a swim, I don't care what you do, just leave me alone."

When Vera made to hang back, Rose pointed towards the door. "You, too. Go! Give me an hour's peace from the lot of you."

The hour's peace never materialized. First to the door, Des gave Rose a long look before turning the knob, and when the door swung wide, the sounds of a commotion in the hallway pushed all thoughts of the last few minutes away.

Chapter Twenty-One

When Rosemary and her friends stepped out into the hallway, it was to find that the cause of the commotion was none other than Charlotte Marlowe. Evidently, she'd remembered where she'd seen the clutch containing the threatening letters, because now she stood at the threshold to her husband's suite, waving the handbag in Geneviève's face while throwing out allegations like rice at a wedding.

"That hideous clutch isn't mine, and even if it were, it doesn't make me a murderer! How dare you come in here and make these—these *accusations ridicules*! Mon Dieu!" Geneviève spat the words at Charlotte, who clenched the hand not holding the clutch into a fist. She appeared poised to pounce on the French woman.

"You're a despicable excuse for a human being! An adulterer and a homewrecker! Why not a blackmailer, and a murderer, too?" Charlotte screeched back.

Geneviève's eyes narrowed, and she held out her hands in a gesture of frustration, "You stupid girl! If I *wrote* the blackmail letters, why would I keep them in my own handbag? À quoi penses-tu?" Again, she reverted to her mother tongue, which Charlotte appeared to get the gist of even if she didn't understand every word.

"I couldn't begin to explain your motives, but then, unlike you, I have scruples!"

While Rosemary and her friends stood back, mouths agape, Geneviève lunged at Charlotte, dragging her into the suite and slamming the door behind her.

Max rushed forward, jiggled the handle, and then looked back at his companions with a furrowed brow. "It's locked," he said. The fight raged on, the women's' voices carrying clearly through the closed door.

"It's not my fault your husband doesn't love you anymore!" Geneviève screamed, aiming the blow right where it would hurt the most.

Charlotte growled with rage and shot back, "He only wants you for your money, and if you haven't figured that out by now, you're even more daft than I thought you were! He's always catting around; always has been a cheat and a liar. He left me with nothing, and he'll do the same to you!"

For a moment, all was silent, and then Geneviève laughed loudly, her voice filled with derision, "Then answer this: why did you want him back so badly?"

"Because!" Charlotte stuttered. "Because I made a vow! He's my husband, for better or for worse. Some people still take marriage seriously! We aren't all tramps like you!"

Rosemary rapped on the door and looked at her friends with wide eyes. "This has nothing to do with Cecily's murder, and it's getting out of hand." Through the door she yelled, "Let us in, right now, or we'll call the police!"

The women inside ignored her demands and continued berating each other. "If you keep insulting me, I'm going to—to rip you apart with my bare hands!" Geneviève's voice had gone past shrill and was now approaching angry desperation. Her threat did nothing to convince Rosemary she wasn't capable of murder, even though her comment on the idiocy of carrying around blackmail letters she'd written herself made a lot of sense.

"Go find Benjamin." She threw the directive over her shoulder. "This is his problem to clean up."

Desmond hastened off to do just that, muttering something under his breath about women being the death of a good man.

For the ten minutes it took Desmond to return with a haggard Benjamin trailing behind, accusations and recriminations flew behind the locked door along with what sounded like at least one crystal bar tumbler that crashed against the wall with a tinkling sound.

Those noises were bad enough, but the utter silence that followed was worse.

"Come on, man," Desmond urged Benjamin. "Open the door, for goodness sake! Your fiancée has gone crazy and is threatening to kill your wife!" Stranger words he had never uttered.

Benjamin's face went white and slack, and then he seemed to get a handle on himself. He fumbled in his pocket for the room key, his hands shaking so much he nearly dropped it, and eventually managed to fit it into the lock. When he finally burst through the door and into the suite, Rosemary and her friends hot on his heels, the scene before him did nothing to calm his nerves.

"Vivi, what on earth are you doing?" he exclaimed. Geneviève had Charlotte on the floor next to the settee, one hand gripping her hair, the other pressing a gleaming steak knife to her throat. On the settee lay a dinner tray, the remainder of its contents having been strewn across the cushion. Had Charlotte arrived sometime later, the dishes might have been cleared, and Geneviève might not have had such a convenient weapon at the ready. "Let her go. It's not her I want, it's you."

"Then why were you with her the night that woman was killed?" Geneviève demanded. "Did you think I didn't know? About her and all your other conquests?"

Benjamin flushed, embarrassed, but didn't take his eyes off his fiancée. "What other conquests? I've been taking care of business, not catting around like everyone thinks. I tried to get Charlotte to agree to petition for a divorce, and yes, I used every means necessary. But I've never hurt you like that, and I never will."

"Are you serious?" Charlotte squeaked around the knife that had gone slack against her throat. Some of the fight seemed to have drained out of Geneviève, and she was now staring at Benjamin as though wondering how many of his words to

139

believe. She tossed the knife aside, and Charlotte scrambled to her feet.

"You still want her, even after she just tried to kill me?" she asked her husband incredulously.

"It's always been her," he stated, not even looking at Charlotte.

Geneviève crossed the space between them and allowed herself to be gathered into Benjamin's arms. "It's only ever been you, too, darling. The rest, it's just—je ne sais quoi—mon ego, je suppose." The two embraced, oblivious to the six other people in the room, especially Charlotte, who stared at them in disgust.

"I think I might be sick," she said, turning a yellowish shade of green.

"I think I might join you," Rosemary agreed. She locked eyes with Charlotte, a long, silent look, and then Charlotte bowed her head.

When she raised it again, there was a steeliness in her eyes that hadn't been there before. "Benjamin, you win. Give me the proof I need, and I'll file the petition immediately. You can have your divorce. I want the money you promised me, and I never want to see either of you ever again."

"That's probably a very wise idea," Max agreed. His tone cut through the haze of romance surrounding Benjamin and Geneviève, and the two split apart reluctantly. "Why don't you two take care of your business elsewhere. Desmond," he said in a harsher tone, "why don't you tag along with them. Frederick, too. Rosemary and I will stay here with Miss Chevalier. It's time we had a conversation."

Benjamin tried to put his hand on Charlotte's waist and lead her out of the suite, but she cringed out of his reach, slapped his hand away, and stalked out in front of him. The men followed, Desmond directing a scathing glare at Max. Rosemary sighed internally; the state of her love life would have to wait. That was a problem for another day.

"Now," Max said when they were safely out of earshot, "you're going to answer any question the lot of us have for you, and you're going to do it truthfully. I could have you arrested for what you've just done, so don't even think about lying."

Rosemary knew Max was putting on more of a show than he needed to and suspected he thoroughly enjoyed doing so.

Geneviève nodded gravely. "Yes, yes. Of course. What do you want to know?" She sat down delicately on the edge of the settee as if she hadn't been holding a knife to someone's throat less than five minutes prior.

"What *I* want to know," Rosemary said loudly, "is where you were the night Cecily was murdered. Clearly, you weren't with your fiancé, as he's just explained he was with his wife." The whole thing sounded so ludicrous, Rose could hardly believe she was asking the question to begin with.

"You still think I killed that woman?" Geneviève had the nerve to ask.

Rosemary sat down on one of the chairs opposite her and glared at the woman. "I think you just proved you're perfectly capable of having done so. Convince us you're innocent, if you can."

"I was here, alone in my suite the evening Cecily DeVant died, waiting for Benjamin."

"Then why did you lie?"

"N'est-ce pas évident?" Geneviève asked. "Because of *you*. All of you. You saw me the night she was killed. Heard the way I spoke to her. I had no alibi, and I'd touched those blackmail letters. Wouldn't you try and save yourself? I may not have liked the woman, but I didn't care enough about her to kill her. Could I take a chance and hope the police would believe me? Perhaps, but I chose not to."

Rosemary exchanged a look with Max, and he watched as the wheels turned in her brain. It was a sight to behold, and one of the things he enjoyed most about her: her mind. "What was your connection to Cecily?" she demanded.

Geneviève sighed, "I had the unfortunate experience of meeting her years ago. We had a row over a man, and she won his affections." She shrugged and rolled her eyes. "It's well over now, and he certainly wasn't someone I cared enough about to make me want to kill her over." Her face smoothed into an innocent, wide-eyed expression.

141

"You mean like you just tried to kill Charlotte?" Vera said pointedly.

Through a laugh, Geneviève's eyes pierced Vera's. "You've never been in love, have you? It has a certain effect on a woman, and sometimes causes one to act brashly."

Vera blanched and promptly shut her mouth.

Even more thoroughly irritated than she'd been before, Rosemary snapped, "Your commentary on my friend's love life is unnecessary, and jealousy is a sorry excuse for threatening someone's life. Enough with this, explain what happened when you returned the handbag to Cecily."

"Mon Dieu! What difference does it make? The bag wasn't hers, as I'd supposed it was. She denied having received those letters, though I didn't believe her for one second. Not after seeing the look on her face when she realized what I'd found, and that I'd seen her sitting in the same chair where I found that hideous handbag."

"What chair? Where?"

"One of those green ones with the silk mohair upholstery in the reception area. We exchanged a few…unpleasantries if you like, and she told me, essentially, to mind my own business and let her handle hers. I was still angry when I saw her at the reception desk that evening. Her indulgent attitude towards her guests did not extend to the ones she did not like, that I can assure you."

At Rose's and Max's insistence, Geneviève ran through her tale twice more, without revealing any inconsistencies, and they were forced to admit she was likely telling the truth. Rose declared she'd like to return to her suite, after of course, checking to ensure there would be no repeat performance of the fight with Charlotte.

Max would have followed Rose to her room, but she gave him a look that said she hadn't yet forgiven him. Vera fared better, as she'd managed to pry the offending clutch from Charlotte and had spread the contents out for perusal. The letters sat off to one side, but it was one item among the rest that held Vera's attention.

The clutch hadn't held much. A small compact, the letters, and a lipstick. Rose sank onto the settee and picked up each item. She opened the compact, then closed it.

"Rose," Vera said. Something about her voice made Rose's head whip in her direction. "I know whose handbag this is."

"How?"

"That shade of lipstick, there's only one person I've seen wearing it. Only one person with the right color of skin to get away with red with a hint of orange. This lipstick belongs to Gloria."

Stunned, Rosemary sat back while the pieces of the puzzle in her mind changed places.

"If the handbag is Gloria's, the letters are hers, too. Do you suppose she was the one stealing money from the hotel?" Vera asked. "It makes a lot of sense, and if Cecily found the letters and confronted her, maybe Gloria killed her to keep her quiet."

Rosemary bit her lip and thought. "Except Cecily didn't have time to talk to Gloria, at least not with the letters on her. She left them here the day she died."

"That doesn't mean she didn't mention them. In fact, it might have benefited her not to have them on her. An insurance policy of sorts."

"Perhaps she thought so, though it didn't keep her from being bludgeoned to death," Rosemary replied. Her throat tightened, and tears threatened to spring to her eyes at the thought. The image of Cecily's body seared into the back of her eyelids, and no matter how many times she blinked, she couldn't stop seeing it. "who do you think wrote the letters?"

Vera opened her mouth, realized she had no answer to that question, and closed it again. "I don't know," she finally admitted, "but it seems as though it would have had to be one of the staff. Someone who figured out what she'd done and threatened to tell Cecily about it."

"It's possible Gloria doesn't even know who sent them," Rosemary said thoughtfully. "It's even possible that Cecily was the one who wrote the letters. It would explain why she brushed off Geneviève's questions—aside, of course, from the obvious

143

fact that she couldn't stand the woman. I hate to think that of her, but we can't rule out the possibility."

"We need to talk to Gloria, don't we?" Vera asked. "I suppose there's no time like the present, but I will say this, Rosie: we're going to need to take a holiday to recover from our holiday."

"Truer words have never been spoken."

Chapter Twenty-Two

Margaret was stationed behind the reception counter, still covering for Gloria after her unfortunate incident that morning. "Margaret," Rosemary said as she approached and rested her elbows on the mahogany surface. "Do you know where Gloria is?"

The girl shook her head. "No, but I assume she's in her cabin, resting." Her eyes narrowed, and she asked, with more edge to her voice they'd never heard before, "Why? Is everything all right?"

"Yes. No. I'm not sure," Rosemary replied, biting her lip and toying with the idea of finding Gloria and wringing her neck.

"What seems to be the trouble?" Benny's voice came from behind Rosemary's shoulder. "I heard a commotion on your floor. Is anyone hurt?"

Rosemary's eyes flicked upwards. "Nothing to worry about, it's all under control. Right now, we need to find Gloria."

"Why? Isn't she well? I thought the doctor said she wasn't badly hurt."

"We think—well, we're worried about her," was all Rose could say.

Vera stepped in, pulling Benny around the corner towards the lift where she assumed was enough privacy to speak candidly.

"We think she might have been the one who stole the register money," she explained to Benny, "and possibly, the one who killed Cecily."

That got Benny's attention, and his face screwed up into a pained, pensive expression. "I can't see why she would kill Miss DeVant after..." he trailed off as usual, further irritating an already frustrated Vera.

"After what, Benny?" Rosemary asked, reaching out to touch him lightly on the arm. The action seemed to rouse him from his reverie.

"Well, the night Cecily died, I heard the two of them talking. I heard Miss DeVant tell Gloria she would help her if she could. Wasn't sure what they were talking about, but Gloria didn't sound angry. She sounded sad. You know, she sends most of her money home to her family in Greece. I think she has a sister who goes to the doctor a lot. Gloria's a nice girl," Benny said, his cheeks pinking.

"Benny, why didn't you tell us this before?" Rosemary wanted to know.

Benny blushed. "Why?" he asked. "Is it important? You never asked about Gloria."

Rosemary sighed for what felt like the hundredth time that day. "No, we didn't, I suppose. We just assumed that because she was also a victim, she couldn't have been the murderer." Her mind began to race, and the pieces of the puzzle started to fall into place.

"It seems as though nearly everyone has been lying about their alibi. Charlotte said she was in her room, but really, she was with Benjamin. Benjamin says he was with Geneviève, but now we know for certain that was also a lie. Richard Wright says he was in his room, and while I doubt that's entirely truthful given his tendency to wander around at all hours of the night, I don't believe he's capable of murder. Then there's you, Benny, who said you were in your cabin all night when really, you were on the beach walking Alfie. Gloria was supposedly on the beach with Walter and—oh!" She stopped abruptly and wished there was a chair behind her to sink into.

"What is it?" Vera asked.

Rosemary explained, "It was windy that night. So windy that it would have been cold on the beach. Not so cold that Benny here would have neglected little Alfie, but windy enough so that a fire wouldn't have stayed lit. Walter and Gloria weren't on the beach that night. Something has always struck me funny about their conversation, and now I know why. They were *both* lying, which means they *both* have something to hide."

Benny still appeared doubtful, but he was starting to worry. "They said they were on the beach?" he asked.

"Yes," Rosemary hedged.

"That spot I told you about, it's Walter's. He likes to take the ladies there to...um...well, you know." What Benny was implying, both Rosemary and Vera understood. "He's always seemed awful keen to know Miss DeVant's plans for the hotel after she retired—"

The conversation was interrupted by the insistent tapping of a finger on Rosemary's shoulder. She whirled around and came face to face with Mrs. Haversham, one of the old biddies who liked to plant themselves in the lounge and watch all the comings and goings.

"Mrs. Lillywhite, we couldn't help overhearing your conversation—" *Of course you could have*, Rosemary thought to herself. "But that lovely little maid of yours, Anna, went off with that man named Walter. I believe he planned to show her his *staff cabin* if you know what I mean." Again, Rosemary understood the insinuation. "We thought it a bit untoward, but it really wasn't our place to pass judgment." *Which you certainly did*, Rosemary thought, though this time she was grateful. "If he's done something wrong, I'd hate to see that sweet girl in any kind of trouble."

"How long ago?" Vera demanded.

"Perhaps a half, maybe three-quarters of an hour ago."

Vera turned to Rosemary, the realization that Anna was alone and possibly poised to lose her innocence to a deranged killer dawning on both of them at the same time.

"We need to let someone know what we're doing," Rosemary said. "Either Max or Freddie or Des. Otherwise, they'll kill us if we haven't got ourselves killed first."

147

"I'll go get them, you take Benny with you," Vera suggested. She strode to the lift, pressed the button, and when nothing happened directed a panicked look at Benny. "We don't have time for this," she said when he raised his hands in a gesture that indicated there wasn't much he could do.

Mrs. Haversham spoke up. "I'll go find your brother and his friends, you run along." How long it might take her to climb the stairs ran through Rosemary's mind, but they were out of options. She made up her mind and stalked across the lobby.

"Benny, are you coming?" Rosemary asked, turning and waving her hand to hurry him along.

He hesitated. "Where did Margaret go? She asked me to check on things upstairs…I don't want to leave without doing my duty." he said, looking around.

"Everything is fine upstairs; maybe Margaret went up to find out for herself." Vera brushed off his concern.

"Still, Cecily said never to leave the lobby unattended."

"Benny, come *on!*" Rosemary pleaded.

Appearing to make up his mind, the porter followed Rosemary out onto the flagstones and towards the beach.

Chapter Twenty-Three

Rosemary and Vera ran as fast as they could down the path towards the beach, Benny huffing and puffing behind them. Veering off in the direction of the staff cabins, Rosemary urged him forward. "Hurry up, Benny. Which cabin is Walter's?"

"Down—down there," he pointed, and Rosemary kicked off her shoes, picking up the pace at the thought of what Walter might be doing to Anna at that very moment.

"Anna!" Rosemary cried, "Anna!" She was getting desperate, her heart threatening to beat out of her chest.

Benny finally caught up to her, and Vera and pointed to the correct cabin. All the windows were dark, but Benny banged his fist on the door anyway. When no sound could be heard from inside, he cast a sideways glance at the women, shook his head, bellowed, and kicked open the door.

"They're not here!" Rosemary exclaimed after a quick search proved the cabin empty. Back outside, the three engaged in a short conversation, unconcerned that their voices carried across the night air. "We have to find them now!"

"Calm down, Rosie," Vera said. "He isn't going to hurt her."

"You don't know that! If he killed Cecily and attacked Gloria, someone he supposedly cared about, we can't be certain about his state of mind."

Vera glanced at the cabin. "We don't have proof he killed Cecily, either. If only we had time to search for the murder weapon. He's probably got it stashed away in there, or somewhere close by."

"We'll have to worry about that later. For now…" Rosemary trailed off when she realized Benny had taken off down the beach. "Benny!" she hollered after him.

"He'll have taken her to his spot. Come on!" Benny urged.

Rosemary slapped her hand to her forehead. "Of course!" she said and took off after him. With Vera bringing up the rear, they caught up to the slower-moving Benny quickly.

"Wait," Vera hissed when they were close enough to see flames flickering from behind the ring of boulders. "The only thing we have on our side is the element of surprise. Go quietly." Because it was good advice, Rose waited until Benny's breathing was less labored, then directed him to take to the shadows.

Raised voices caused the hair on Rosemary's arms to lift as she crept slowly forward.

"Don't you dare move a muscle!" The voice carrying across the sea air proved to be neither Anna's nor Walter's. Wedging herself between two of the boulders she knew would allow her a view of the fire ring without betraying her presence, Rosemary chanced a peek.

Her mouth dropped open in surprise when she saw Margaret standing next to the fire brandishing a knife, her eyes wild and her face a mask of anger. *Isle of Love, my left eye*, thought Rosemary. *More like the Isle of Crazy Women Wielding Knives*.

Margaret glared daggers at the two figures across the fire.

Now that Rosemary had a decent vantage point, she could see Anna pressed against the very boulder she'd declared would be a lovely spot from which to watch the sunset. The kimono Anna had borrowed from Vera was now wrinkled but still intact, though the girl's makeup was smudged and her hair a disheveled mess. The frightened expression on her face made Rosemary want to jump up from her hiding spot and rip Margaret to pieces.

"We have to get her out of there," Rosemary whispered.

"There's a way around. See that clump of scrub brush?" Benny pointed towards a shadowed space that none of the group had noticed the first time they'd explored the area.

"I'll go that way," Vera said, her mouth set in a thin line. "Benny, you go around the front, cover her flank in case she tries to lunge." She pointed towards the water's edge, which, with the tide out, had receded enough to allow access, just as Frederick had postulated. "Wait for my signal, and then take her down," she instructed Benny, then nodded at Rosemary and began to hedge her way towards the path while Margaret continued to spit venom.

The receptionist snarled at Walter and spat, "How dare you bring her here? To *our* special spot."

Rosemary would have laughed, had the situation not been so dire, at the notion that Margaret believed she was the only woman Walter had ever seduced in this place.

With an almost audible click sounding on Rosemary's head, the rest of the puzzle fell into place. Or almost all of them.

"Margaret, please," Walter pleaded, "she means nothing to me. *You're* the one I want." Despite his panic, he sounded insincere.

Margaret, however, only seemed to hear the words rather than the emotion behind them and softened infinitesimally. Rosemary could see Vera getting closer to where Anna was huddled while Benny got into position and felt a surge of hope shoot through her.

It fizzled into nothing about ten seconds later when Gloria came careening down the path and inserted herself into the fight between Walter and Margaret.

"You killed Miss DeVant!" she screeched at Walter, whose face turned even whiter in the flickering light of the fire. "And you attacked me, didn't you?" she demanded. Rosemary realized too late that the conversation between herself, Vera, and Benny back at the staff cabins had reached Gloria's ears.

"She's the one holding the knife, and you think *I'm* the murderer?" Despite the gravity of the situation, Walter stared at Gloria as if she'd lost her faculties and let out a short bark of a laugh. "But you're the one put in charge of the hotel. Boggles the mind."

"Stop talking to her," Margaret said, coming even further unhinged. "Of course, Walter wasn't the one who attacked you, Gloria. *That* was me. You should have listened when I told you to stay away from him!"

That startled Gloria, who turned her attention to Margaret. Rosemary hunkered further down between the boulders, still hidden from view. Gloria was the only one who could see her, and with her attention focused elsewhere, she had no reason to expose Rosemary's presence. While the argument raged on, Rose waited for an opening to disarm Margaret and hoped Vera had managed to get close enough to rescue Anna before things got any further out of control.

"What are you talking about, Margaret?" Gloria asked. "Were you and Walter involved with each other? I had no idea."

"I sent you those letters!" Margaret screeched. "I told you to leave me what's mine and that you'd pay if you didn't listen!"

Rosemary groaned internally. This whole time, she'd been chasing a dead end. The so-called blackmail notes had nothing to do with the money, or with Cecily or her death—at least not directly. They were merely the ravings of a scorned lover. It seemed Geneviève and Benjamin weren't the only love-crazed couple who deserved one another. Walter and Margaret were cut from the same cloth.

"You're insane, the both of you!" Gloria said, voicing Rosemary's thoughts out loud.

Walter tried once more to backtrack. "I ended things with Margaret a month ago!" he tried to put even more distance between them, but Margaret inched closer. "And what happened to Miss DeVant was an accident!"

"You *accidentally* picked up a doorstop and bashed her over the head with it?" Gloria retorted. "How stupid do you think I am? I suppose all the time you spend chasing girls who are too young to realize what a cad you are has made you think we're all idiots!"

"No, that's not what happened at all," he said, rushing to defend himself. "I didn't know Cecily was in the supply cupboard at all. Charlotte kept leaving the door open, and I assumed she'd done it again. I was annoyed with her, so I gave the door a hard shove on my way past. It hit Cecily and knocked her down. When I saw her lying on the floor, I knew I'd be fired, so I panicked and closed the door. She's dead, and it's my fault, but I didn't mean to kill her."

Benny finally hit his limit just as Vera whistled out her signal, popped up behind Walter, and tackled him to the ground. "She was my friend!" he yelled, "and you killed her over your stupid job!"

It looked as though Benny was going to return the favor until Rosemary stood up from where she was crouched and yelled, "Benny, stop, he's not worth it! It won't bring Cecily back!"

"Yes, Benny," Margaret growled. "you should listen to your meddlesome friend. Besides, Walter didn't kill Cecily. I did."

The puzzle pieces Rosemary had been juggling to fit together finally clicked into place. "Walter knocked Cecily out, but you came along behind him and finished her off. Why, Margaret? Why would you kill someone who'd treated you with kindness?"

"I did it for Walter." She turned to him, and in the flickering firelight, he shivered at the madness he saw on her face. "I did it for you. Did you know Cecily owned this place? I heard her laughing about Mr. Wright and his attempts to purchase the hotel. The stupid man, she said, had no idea he was already talking to the owner, and she had no intention of selling. Not ever."

"That's no reason to kill her," Walter said. "I don't understand."

"Don't you?" Margaret's voice shrilled. "With her alive, you'd never get promoted to manager. She wasn't going to retire, and she wasn't going to sell. With her out of the way, you can have her job, and her salary, and we can get married."

From the horrified look on Walter's face, the prospect of marriage was more frightening than knowing someone had killed in his name. Still, his apparent innocence did little to assuage Benny's fury, but Walter made no attempt at defense when the young porter swung a fist.

153

Vera had taken the opportunity to try and rescue Anna, but Margaret caught sight of her and deftly grabbed hold of Anna's hair with one hand, the knife still held firmly in the other. "Sit back down," she spat at Vera who, with a glance at Rosemary, did as she was told.

Rose watched as Margaret hauled Anna closer to where Benny was still pummeling Walter. "Stop," she said, kicking at Benny. "Leave him alone, or you'll have another body on your hands." She pulled at Anna's hair, causing the girl to cry out. "Shut up," Margaret said, and wrapped her arm around Anna's throat in a chokehold, squeezing tightly enough to make her gasp for air.

It was a standoff, with Rosemary too afraid to approach, Vera pressed against the boulder, and Benny holding Walter down. Gloria looked around as though she wasn't quite sure how she'd got herself into this mess and began to back away.

"Don't move," Margaret said, squeezing even tighter when Benny released Walter and prepared to lunge at her. That stopped Benny in his tracks, and he mimicked Gloria by backing off.

"What do you want from us?" Rosemary asked, a plea in her voice. "Let her go, and we'll let you go." To that, Benny grunted, and Rosemary shot him a quelling look. Anna's face had begun turning purple. Time was running out.

Margaret considered her options, but when Anna went slack in her arms, she realized she'd taken too long to decide. Unable to hold onto the dead weight of Anna's body and the knife at the same time, she let the girl fall and took a few steps back, pointing the blade in Benny's direction.

Anna crumpled, landing face down in the sand, and didn't move. Rage welled up in Rosemary's throat; rage and sadness, but there was no way for her to get to Anna while Margaret still held all the power.

"Put the knife down," came a voice from behind Rosemary. She turned and was flooded with relief at the sight of Max, Frederick, and Desmond coming down the path from the hotel.

Max pointed his gun at Margaret and pulled back the hammer. "Now." She looked around, realized she'd brought a knife to a gunfight, and threw the weapon to the ground.

Frederick rushed forward, and when he saw Anna's prone figure in Vera's kimono, turned white as a sheet. "No, no, no!" He dropped to his knees beside her, and in the lowering light, Rose could see how he might mistake their identities.

He fell to his knees, calling out endearments he would never have let pass his lips if he thought Vera could hear them and reached to turn Anna over.

A hand fell on his shoulder, and Freddie looked up at Vera's smiling face.

Freddie gave a start, then looked down at Anna as Rosemary shoved him aside to check for a pulse.

"She's alive." Anna pulled in a breath and her eyelids fluttered as Rose tenderly brushed her hair back from her eyes.

Freddie knew nothing of the rest, as Vera's hand slid from his shoulder to cup his chin and urge him to stand. Words failed him as the woman he never knew he wanted moved close, then closer still. "Did you mean any of that?" she asked. "Those things you said, did you mean them?"

"Every word." His breath tickled her lips. Her breath quickened, and then she was in his arms, crushed so close that their bodies felt like one. "Vera," he whispered and lowered his head for a kiss that nearly set his hair on fire.

"Well, it's about time," Anna croaked through a throat raw from her ordeal.

"Yes, Anna, it is," Rosemary agreed.

Chapter Twenty-Four

Inspector Boothe and his team had arrived minutes later and promptly arrested Margaret. The murder weapon having been found in her cabin shortly thereafter effectively sealed her fate. Walter argued his innocence to anyone who would listen. Still in charge, Gloria promptly relieved him of his position even though Boothe declined to bring charges against him.

Now, two days later, Rosemary and her friends sat around one of the tables in the lounge and prepared for their departure from Cyprus. None amongst them desired to finish out their stay at The Aphrodite, particularly Anna, who had opted to have breakfast sent to the suite rather than face being pelted with questions by curious guests.

Richard Wright hunched in a chair to their left, and though he'd nodded once in Rosemary's direction, he'd been uncharacteristically quiet since Margaret's arrest.

"It looks like Benjamin and Geneviève had the same idea we did," Rosemary commented as she watched Benny wheel their luggage out of the lobby to a bus waiting at the curb. They still appeared besotted with one another, and Rose merely shook her head at the thought of what their future might hold. "And good riddance."

"You never know, Rosie," Vera said, turning her attention away from Frederick. "They might spend the rest of their lives together, happy as clams."

Her opinion raised both of Rosemary's eyebrows. "Since when did you become an optimist?" she quipped, her gaze darting from Vera to Frederick.

"Recently, I suppose," she winked at her friend and elbowed Freddie in the ribs.

"I give it a month, tops," he said with a snort, earning himself a narrow-eyed glare followed by a kiss that demanded the rest of the group avert their eyes.

At least Rosemary only had to concern herself with her own love life now, though the thought of confronting that situation made her stomach churn. "I wonder what Boothe is doing here," she said, her attention, for the moment, having been captured by the sight of the inspector escorting a balding man in a natty suit across the lobby.

He approached Benny, and after a brief conversation, the two went into the hotel office and shut the door behind them.

"He's probably tying up loose ends," Max explained. "I think he's still mildly irritated that you solved the case before he could."

"I can't take the credit for this one," Rosemary said. Nor did she want to. "I was certain Mr. Wright was the murderer, and then nearly as certain of both Gloria and Walter. Benny is the one entitled to the glory. If he hadn't been there, and if you three hadn't arrived...well, I don't know what might have happened."

"Sometimes, Rose, it's not about the glory," Max replied. "Sometimes it's about legwork. You can't speak as to what would have become of Anna had she been left alone with Walter and Margaret. You probably saved her life. Let's call it a group effort."

When, sometime later, Benny emerged from the office behind Inspector Boothe, he wore a smile that contrasted starkly with his red-rimmed, watery eyes. Both of them approached the table where Rosemary and her friends were finishing up breakfast.

"I wanted you to be the first to know," Benny said, shifting from one foot to the other, barely able to contain his emotions, "that I'm the new owner of The Aphrodite." He let the revelation sink in, as much for himself as anyone else.

Inspector Boothe introduced his companion, who turned out to be the executor of Cecily's will. At Benny's insistence, Mr. Cardington-Vale revealed the reason he had come all the way to Cyprus.

Cecily DeVant had a son. A baby she'd named Ben. A baby born out of wedlock and raised by a married but childless friend. Benny knew the woman who raised him hadn't been his real mother, but he'd had no idea the woman he'd known as Aunt Cecily was blood to him.

"That has to be the saddest thing I've ever heard of," Vera said, a tear threatening to form in the corner of her eye. This time, it had nothing to do with her bout of the sniffles, and everything to do with her soft heart.

"Not for me, Miss," Benny said softly. "I thought my mother had died long ago. I'd made peace with the fact that I'd never see her or know her. But I did get to know her. She left me a whole box of letters along with her share of the hotel. The Aphrodite is mine now."

Mr. Cardington-Vale would stay on for a few months to help Benny come to terms with his new life. When Richard Wright heard the news, he packed his bags in record time and pressed Inspector Boothe into offering him a lift. He seemed anxious to shake himself loose from the Aphrodite as quickly as possible.

Satisfied he'd done his duty by all concerned, Boothe gave Rosemary one long look and then turned on his heel. The last she heard from him was a low-voiced, and not especially complimentary, comment about lady detectives.

The End

Made in the USA
Coppell, TX
30 July 2020